# ALL THAT WAS ASKED

VANESSA MACLAREN-WRAY

Cover design copyright © 2023 by Kelley York
*sleepyfoxstudio.net*

Published by Water Dragon Publishing
*waterdragonpublishing.com*

An imprint of Paper Angel Press
*paperangelpress.com*

ISBN 978-1-959804-84-0 (Trade Paperback)

10 9 8 7 6 5 4

SECOND EDITION

*For Alan, of course.*

# ACKNOWLEDGEMENTS

T HIS, MY VERY FIRST PUBLISHED BOOK, was released at the outset of the COVID-19 pandemic. It was a fascinating—and frustrating—time to enter the world of publishing. Like everyone else, I did my best to pivot to the internet universe and found ways to do readings and interact online. I want to thank my old friends at BayCon for including me in the mini-cons they hosted and new friends at Octocon, DisCon III, and the Nebula Conference for welcoming me as a volunteer and participant.

Thanks to the California Writers Club (South Bay and SF Peninsula chapters) I learned to run Zoom gatherings (and keep attendees safe from Zoom-bombers), attended online workshops, and developed on-screen presentation skills. I kept working on new material, which benefited from critique through two online circles: the San Mateo Science Fiction and Fantasy Meetup and the East Bay Science Fiction and Fantasy Writers. And, yes, I relished mic-off companionable work hours through *Shut Up and Write*. (Hey, now: Audrey Kalman, Chris Kalaboukas, Lisa Meltzer Penn … I'm talking at you, here! Wait, wait, am I muted again?)

As we emerge from those deep pandemic times—and as the sequel to *All That Was Asked* emerges into this transformed world—Steven Radecki (aka Water Dragon Publishing) offered to bring out a fresh edition. Mostly, we're updating the cover to connect it with the other Patchwork Universe books. So, if you've already bought this book—thank you, but you don't need a second copy … except you do, don't you? Isn't this cover to die for? (Kelley York's studio is right on the copyright page, if you're looking for a book cover designer. Just sayin'.)

None of that has overwritten the gratitude expressed in the first edition. I owe so much to the members of the Morgan Hill Writers Group—our local critique circle, which moved online in 2019. Kris Miller and Walter von Tagen III endured the evolution of every single chapter from start to finish. Kris shares my love of words, but knew when to tell me to cut the technobabble and fix the structure. Walter helped curb my tendency to ramble along on some tangent and even convinced me to change the title. Susan Nicolson was a steady source of encouragement as I was looking for a path to publishing. In exchange, I had the pleasure of reading their stories ... long before anyone else.

I suppose one isn't typically expected to thank a publisher, other than by writing a profitable book, but this is a special case. Steven Radecki opened the door wide, letting me make far more than the usual adjustments to the standard Paper Angel Press contract, thus making me feel much more like a partner in this production than I ever might have done. (And that's continued to this day ... I get to be on his podcast, we've created workshops together, he's helped me learn marketing ... within my limited scope in that arena.)

The BayCon community has continued to be a lifeline, welcoming me into the organized chaos that is our San Francisco Bay Area SFF convention. Ashley Fakava and Susie Rodriguez, especially, have done more than they know to make me feel like a real human being with a place in this world. (That too, wasn't eroded by pandemic days. Returning to in-person BayCon in 2022 involved a lot of happy tears.)

Throughout, my family somehow put up with both literal and virtual absences, as I vanished into my cluttered office to hammer away on this ancient computer or dash off to (or log in for) another convention or critique-circle meeting. My husband, Alan Wray, has continued to take on chores I was meaning to do—and encourage taking time off as well—but I haven't forgotten that he proofread this manuscript, critiqued supporting materials, and wielded the camera when I had to come up with a photograph. My grown sons, Corwin, Addien, and Tirion, provide regular doses of support while continually exposing me to new ideas about the way the world works, new ways of thinking about people, and new kinds of storytelling.

I wish it wasn't true that my parents are gone, but I will always thank them for setting things in motion. My mother, Lorraine MacLaren, made sure there were books in our house—including a set of encyclopedias to browse through, before the internet changed research forever. My father, William G. MacLaren, Jr., introduced me to science fiction and computers, and he conspired to sneak SF books from the regular section of the library when I exhausted the supply in the juvenile section. Throughout their lives, each in their own way, my parents demonstrated the importance of taking action when someone needs help, especially if that someone is seen by others as an outsider ... a stranger ... an alien.

# ALL THAT WAS ASKED

# 1



*"I knew it was a person the moment it came screaming out of the woods. But I had to have my little bit of fun with young Ansegwe."*

– Eskenyan Jemenga
Physician

P OETRY MAY BE MY FIRST LOVE, but the events of my first Transfer Expedition brought about such changes in my life I can hardly see myself that far in the past. My stores of delicately-constructed stanzas cannot help me; rather, I must call upon that most acute aid to memory: pain.

After three months of marching through the wilderness, I had forgotten poetry and knew only my own personal agonies.

The pains in my terminal pads began as individual ripping snags, as if every vestigial sucker beneath the surface had sprouted hooks. As time wore on, those stabbing points of fire expanded and merged forces, so that I plodded along on four wads of torment. Meanwhile, the incessant rubbing of my inexpertly-adjusted pack grated the flesh on my back until a broad, thick callus decorated the crest of my hind end—that part of my anatomy that had formerly been deemed so attractive to the opposite sex. Their spring-muscles exhausted by endless startle responses, my spines ached ferociously. Even worse, at the microscopic level my skin crawled with foreign bacteria and bloodthirsty parasites, each triggering its own exquisitely unforgettable tactile sensations. Meanwhile, should I even dare think of home, my intestinal tract cramped and rumbled ferociously, declaring its revulsion to our steady diet of hardtack and mashed reconstituted vegetable-based protein.

The Varayla Ansegwe who'd set out with poetry at his fingertips, declaiming excitedly at every turn of the trail, constructing appropriate verses as each new vista presented itself, had become a distant memory. After weeks of trudging at the tail end of the company, my mouth stayed shut and my elegant expressive fingers remained curled out of the way of my grasping digits. Admittedly, my companions suffered even more greatly, as their mission—which I served as merely an unwanted tag-along— could only be described as an utter failure. We limped back to base with far too little to show for my family's extravagant investment in the venture.

Granted, the mapping process had proceeded without incident, but we hadn't discovered any territory more remarkable than the unimaginatively-named 'Deep Valley' itself—the start point for every authorized Transfer Expedition to this so-called parallel universe. The landscapes our expedition encountered paled by comparison with the stunning Deep Valley, and our map entries served only to corroborate reports from previous explorers.

None of the other expedition projects could share even the modest satisfaction the map-makers obtained from completing their minimum-objectives checklist. Geologist Kulandere hauled a pack loaded with rocks, but none represented anything more than a material reference keyed to the baseline geologic survey. She'd found no new minerals—let alone the veins of precious ores promised in the expedition prospectus. Similarly, Physician Jemenga's biological samples catalogued only the mundane, with no fascinating new alien animals, plants, or fungi to report.

Least impressive of all, the so-called Contact Crew—to whose mission I was supposedly attached—had not even found an opportunity to observe the so-called Stick Men, let alone to conduct our carefully planned, totally controlled, culturally sanitized meeting. The other two members of my team made it abundantly clear that they considered my presence to have been unlucky. So much for the objective scientific viewpoint.

With every inflammation-enhancing step, I knew more and more surely that Aunt Ansele and Aunt Adeleke's decision to force the crew to include their college-boy nephew served as a punishment, not a career-building move. Not that participating had been in any way my own idea. Building a career was never high on my priority list. It ranked well below poetry (of course), courting brilliant female students, playing ball, and even dragging out the education process. Contrary to the old ladies' impression, I did enjoy university, even the coursework. It's just that I felt no need to pursue any particular line of study; let us say instead that I preferred to browse the canopy of the tree of knowledge.

On the outward trek, I had indulged in admiring the scenery. The forest exuded romance—an ancient wilderness defined by rank upon rank of tremendous conifers towering over copses of pretty little deciduous trees that glittered tantalizingly in the sunlight. I had eagerly composed little poems in my head and jotted them down when granted free time during halts. As for everything else that gave me pleasure, this activity earned heartfelt ridicule from the authentic members of the expedition. They were not even impressed when I took the time to inspect the glitter trees more closely, to discover that their leaves—pale on the undersides—hung upon flexible stems, so that the leaves shivered in the slightest breeze, flashing those pale undersides towards the light. What benefit derived from an explanation for a merely aesthetic effect, the others complained, when I'd single-handedly delayed the day's journey?

While the forest we trekked through obstructed potential vistas of distant peaks or nearby valleys, there were other sights that went unappreciated by my compatriots. Where slopes tilted more steeply, the forest was broken by long, near-vertical open stretches giving play to rich green meadow grasses and intensely bright flowers. The flowers drew the eye with fantastic patterns etched in glittering iodic purples, those high-frequency wavelengths so easily seen and so tricky to capture in a photograph. I enjoyed pausing at these junctures to take in the views, but Kulandere unromantically proclaimed those open spaces to be avalanche chutes and pointed to the stumps of shattered trees as evidence.

It was at the base of one of these dangerously steep hillsides that the tedium was finally broken. We had been granted a break, ordered to rest in the protective shade of the trees. As usual, I was daydreaming, disobeying my superiors in order to bask in the afternoon sunlight slanting through the edge of the canopy.

Abruptly, from upslope, I heard shouts.

I think I had the dim notion that some member of our party had gone exploring up there, so I stepped out to wave the supposed stragglers to our hidden position. If I had been thinking instead of dreaming, perhaps I would have noticed the shouts were not those of my people. Instead, I found myself alone and in plain view of the primitives we'd been seeking for so long and with such circumspection.

I no longer wondered if we might somehow have accidentally failed to notice the Stick Men; such creatures we could not have missed. These particular specimens were vocalizing loudly while waving either tools or weapons. Alarmingly, they were only a hundred strides or so away, though uphill. A total of six of the small four-limbed bipeds stared down at me. Two had somehow affixed themselves to the backs of much larger bony quadrupeds. Their hides—or clothing—blended with the soft brown coats of the beasts they rode. The ultimate effect was that of a pair of strangely misshapen persons, consistent with the early reports that had drawn us out on this expedition.

To this day, I am not sure if the Stick Men ever actually saw me. My philosophy mentor insists that they visually perceived but failed to conceptualize my actual presence, because to them my appearance could be only an unacceptable anomaly. In fact, Tkonle argues I was invisible, "concealed by the cloak of cognitive disconnection." This is all a bit much for my pedestrian way of thinking, but it is true that they did not react to my presence. One would have expected cries of surprise—or even screams of horror. However, for my part, I would have been satisfied if they had simply fled over the hill.

At the time, however, the Stick Men and I were all focused on something other than one another. There was a third factor in play: something else was crashing its way down the slope, taking a noisy, sliding route just inside the tree line on the opposite side of the avalanche path. This gave me the impression that I had encountered a hunting party. Perhaps, I thought, I might prove my worth to the expedition by making some sensible observations of this activity. At the same time, I fervently wished there were some way I could catapult my handsome callused backside—not to mention the rest of my person—back into concealment.

Luckily, the Stick Men remained intent on their prey, which burst out of cover very near the bottom of the slope, opposite my exposed position. I expected to see one of the delicate little browsers that we had encountered numerous times, or possibly one of those slinky brush-tailed predators—in which case I might be able to document these people as herders defending domesticated flocks.

Instead, the creature dashing towards me resembled the Stick Men, being at least partially bipedal, though it went on all fours much of the time. However, rather than that friendly shade of brown, its hide was practically colorless, though its eyes were dark.

The Stick Men let out more of their incomprehensible noises as soon as they spotted the pale creature. I felt a queasy distaste at the idea that they would hunt a creature so obviously close to their evolutionary line of descent. For a moment, I questioned my hypothesis that they were hunting. My doubts evaporated when a projectile speared the earth so close to me that I could see soil puff into the air when the weapon struck. I expected the animal to startle at the missile and dodge back into the forest primeval. To my surprise, it labored onward, and my alarm redoubled, for its path lay directly towards me.

There was nothing for it. I gathered myself for what I was sure would be a completely visible, incompletely successful, spring back to my comrades in the shadows. But then the animal began making noises, high-pitched squealing sounds, and I was distracted enough to turn back towards it.

Most alarmingly, the animal had adjusted its path and, instead of veering away, it aimed itself precisely in my direction. As it ran, it kept rising up from its four-footed scramble, sliding on the loose soil, and ululating crazily. If it had been a large animal, or even a small one with sharp teeth, I might have screamed myself. But it was clearly a non-predatory beast, revealing only flat, grazing-animal teeth as it howled. The thin, clawless forefeet it thrashed in the air indicated its charge was only a sham display. Perhaps it had young nearby to defend. I stood my ground, quelled my impulse to gesture for help, and kept silent. With any luck, the thing would dodge at the last moment and plunge into the forest behind me, making it then the problem of my so-called teammates.

Another projectile landed, this one nearly at my feet. Belatedly, I remembered the other potential threat in the field. I hesitated. (Oh, the slow-as-mud thinking of the young!) Should I draw my staser? Would it frighten them off or make them angrier? Or should I make a run for it and draw their fire directly?

As always, when one party hesitates, the other takes the initiative. Into that gap sprang the colorless creature. It leaped past the second spear, launching itself into a sliding dive that ended with it clutching my talus so tightly the foot below ceased its insistent throbbing. I stopped breathing and stared down in genuine horror as it clambered its way halfway up my leg. The thing continued shrieking, but now released one set of claws and aimed that forelimb towards the Stick Men, stretching one digit out, for all the world like a person pointing out an item of interest. The pursuers had abandoned their steeds and began furiously skid-sliding down the slope, still shouting. Frantic, I looked back and forth between the hunters hefting their weapons and the creature attached to my forelimb.

In that moment, as easily as sliding a new lens into place on one of Jemenga's infernal microscopes, I saw the prey clearly. It was not howling like an animal; it was jabbering like a person in peril. It was talking, and it was talking to me. Clearly, it had a great deal that it desired to communicate to me regarding the Stick Men. Were there two potentially intelligent species here? And how was it that one seemed oblivious to me, while the other not only recognized me as a person and, further, was determined make contact and convince me to protect it from its pursuers?

In that moment of epiphany, my reactions were not well thought out. I suppose I might have shouted something to scare off the Stick Men. Surely simply drawing their attention to my physical appearance would have served nicely. But no, not Ansegwe, proud scion of the notorious Family Varayla. I snapped the staser out of my front pocket and gave the Stick Men a quick jolt of electric-shock-via-ultraviolet-ionization. Contrary to the concerns expressed in the Contact Handbook, this did not seem to accelerate the Stick Men's technological advancement, but it did result in their falling senseless into the undergrowth.

"Now!" barked Alekwa. "Games are over! They will not be down for long! Move out!"

And the company, as usual, leaped to obey. All but me.

"Ansegwe!" she shouted. "Shake off that thing and get moving."

I craned my head around to peer uncertainly at Tekere, my Contact Crew leader. "But isn't this what we're here for?" I said, plaintively. "Isn't this Contact?"

He shook his coiled right arm at me, purple with exasperation. "This is not Contact! This is blundering! Incompetent contamination of data! Violation of protocols! Who knows how long it will take to overcome this setback?" With his left hand, he uncoiled his expressive fingers and underlined his public comments with a personally-offensive set of parallel remarks, for my eyes only.

"Oh." I could feel myself paling in embarrassment and shame. Once again, Ansegwe the Outsider makes a mess of things. I looked down at the creature now crumpled at my feet.

Breathing rapidly, it stared back to where the Stick Men had fallen. Then it glanced up at me, now confident in its safety, and released its grip on my leg. I couldn't explain myself. There was no real evidence. It just looked intelligent. Surely only a fool would walk away now. But I was merely baggage ... foolish baggage.

I stepped back carefully, quietly. It rose up to its hind legs; well, maybe it was really bipedal after all. Still, it stared at me, unafraid. I couldn't help myself.

"Good-bye, then," I said, for all the world as if I was talking to a person I'd bumped into on the street at home. "Sorry we can't stay and chat."

Continuing to not think at all, I reached out one hand as if expecting it to mesh fingertips like a civilized person. But it did reach out its forepaw, which had long-fingered hands, like a rodent—or a person—and our fingers did touch, just barely. It was an electric moment. I felt as if I'd dosed myself with the staser, instead of the Stick Men.

# 2

*"At first, we were all nervous about having a Syndicate family member embedded in the crew. But Ansegwe was such a noof, always with his head in the sky and his feet in the mud."*

– Nara Ensargen
Contact Crew

M Y NERVES STILL QUIVERING WITH ELECTRICITY, I turned to look for Tekere, to ask more advice, only to see the last of the team already fading into the woods. No time left, unless I wanted all the time in the world, alone.

"Wait!" I called out.

Moving automatically, I trotted over to my pack, slung it into position, and hustled along their track. All the while, my mind was full of the image of that moment. I didn't care what the others thought. We had Made Contact. There would be something to talk about at home now.

Shortly, I managed to catch up with one of the other younger team members, Ensargen, who'd been assigned to bring up the rear. For once, he was willing to commiserate with me as we trudged along. Apparently, open disobedience of a team leader and smashing expedition protocols were a ticket to acceptance in the rebel generation.

For about a quarter of an hour, I felt almost like a real team member. Then my new partner looked over his shoulder and said, "Well."

The creature was following us.

This was certainly not in the Project Plan. I glanced nervously ahead at the seniors. Had anyone else noticed? The spindly little character was small and probably tired from being chased, but we were all loaded down with expedition gear. It was actually gaining on us. I tried taking a few steps back and making what I hoped were fearsome gestures. Clearly, I was awful at being awful; the creature perked up and hurried along faster, gesturing in return. I toyed with the idea of stasing it, but my partner-of-the-moment snagged my arm. We had lost ground and jogged to catch up.

Meanwhile, of course, everyone had noticed.

"Taking something home for the maiden aunts?"

"Look, Ansegwe's finally collected something!"

"Bets on when it'll catch up?"

"Bets on which limb it'll attack this time?"

I had to suck in a deep lungful of air to keep my temper. Both aunts had laid it on very thick: the consequences of one of my infamous blow-ups would be equivalent to not returning from the trip. I plodded on, keeping my eyes on the feet in front of me. But then the commentary shifted suddenly.

"Well, that's that. Don't cry, now, little Ans'we."

"Who bet on 'never'?"

I risked a look back. The creature had stopped. It seemed to be in some new kind of distress. It had lost coordination; its limbs jerked and twisted until it fell to the ground. It crawled a little distance, then pushed itself to its feet again. From my comrades' comments, it seems that had not been its first fall. But the next time, it did not rise. Even from this distance, I could see that its torso and limbs continued to spasm. Clearly, it had been struck previously by the hunters and was now finally succumbing to its wounds.

Meanwhile, the troop was moving on, nearly out of sight already. Once again, I had to trot to catch up, the pack banging ruthlessly. We were back on track. There would be no more damage to protocol and planning. Three more days, then baths unlimited!

I expected to feel relief, that easing of attention that comes when a predator stalking the party loses interest and turns aside. This time, there came no such release; rather, my attention was riveted behind us. I willed my ears forward, but they rebelled. Instead of the soft chatter of the team ahead, I heard only the gasping nonsense farther and farther behind. Even as I consciously directed myself to think ahead, to phrase out the beginnings of my expeditionary report, all my best neurons were devoted to puzzling out the word-like utterances of the creature back there.

*Waiwai eymcumm wai can t'movma fit owwoww eywl ono estop.*

I found myself walking slower and slower. I swear I could not help myself. Not when I stopped entirely. Not even when I turned from the group and started back. And it was then … then that I felt relief, as if released from a trap. My strides grew long, rolling into a comfortable three-beat lope, bringing me back to the downed creature in nearly no time at all.

When it saw me, it fell silent, and its thrashing efforts to rise ceased. But I observed that its limbs still jerked and twitched spasmodically. It breathed hard, as if afraid. Yet when I reached towards it, the creature did not draw back from me. Rather, it returned the gesture, stretching out both forelimbs to me, despite the random quakes and jerks. I wondered at my own lack of fear; but then again, I couldn't smell any warning signs of disease or of aggression.

So, when it actually grasped my outstretched hand, I found it not too difficult to restrain the instinct to pull away. Its skin felt cool to the touch, and its angular, many-jointed fingers pinched somewhat. The physical contact seemed to calm it slightly, as its respiration grew slower. I could even feel a pulse in its fingertips—a flutter that slowed from a feverish racing pace to a more measurable one.

I was struck by a foolish impulse to pick up the thing and carry it. That would not have been difficult; I estimated its mass at well under a fourth of my own. Still, I had attended to our lessons during the required emergency medical training sessions. The creature's involuntary motions bespoke neurological trouble. Perhaps it had suffered a brain or neural injury, in which case abrupt movement could damage it further. Proceeding quietly and gently, I disengaged my hand, stood, and curled my fingers to form a trumpet.

"Jemenga!" I called forward.

Far up the trail, about to disappear in a thickening of the trees, I saw the group stop. I waved my arm vigorously and could see that at least I had their attention. One of the youngsters began to sprint back down the track, the low man elected to make the run back to find out what crazy Ansegwe was up to now.

About halfway, he stopped and hollered, "What is it, now?"

"Get me Jemenga!" I bellowed back. "I need the medic!"

Without further noise, he pelted back. There was a fair amount of discussion; I could tell even from that distance. Though his back was turned, I could pick out Jemenga's iridescent green bag … and his long black arms gesticulating angrily. Finally, he turned and trudged towards me. I braced myself for a row. But he walked slowly, shifting the medical kit from one hand to another as he came.

By the time he arrived, the anger was gone. He had used the time well. Less well than I had, of course. For I had done no thinking at all, had merely enjoyed the sensation of rising hope as he approached. I believe I even indulged myself in telling the uncomprehending creature that help was on the way. As soon as Jemenga came in easy earshot, I began.

"Thank you, Jemenga. I am so grateful. What do you think you can do for our little follower here?"

But he barely looked at it, jerking and moaning so pitiably at his very feet. Instead, he set the bag down, put his arm across my back, and turned me away to face the woods.

"Ansegwe," he said calmly. "I know you are the expedition sponsors' nephew …"

"Yes, yes, but I am not asking as Varayla Ansegwe. You know I wouldn't play those games. Haven't I been a good member of the group?"

He huffed a little, the closest I'd yet heard to a laugh from him. "Ha-hm. Lad, you have tried, but it is a little difficult for others to forget. But you have been well-educated, have you not?"

With that, he moved in front of me, one limber hand on each of my shoulders, both deep eyes gazing authoritatively into my own. It was a little daunting, I can tell you. Even then, Jemenga was a formidable person.

"Um, yes, at least I study well enough. No one would call me a brilliant student. But I generally do better than passing." I was still puzzled. There are some consequences to youth, most of them involving the inability to follow a good line of thought to its logical conclusion.

"You know my vows, then," he said.

"Um, yes, I think." But of course, I had to think rather hard, and he watched my progress critically.

"*For the wild …*" he prompted.

"Yes, yes. *For the wild beast, respect and freedom from even compassion. For the beast in our care, freedom from pain and …* er …"

He squeezed my shoulders encouragingly. It came to me.

"*… release from fear. For the person, all that is asked.* Yes, yes, but what has that got to do with … with …" As I fumbled for words, the doctor turned me gently round until once again we were standing side to side, with his avuncular arm looped over my shoulders.

"Son, is this a person?"

I swallowed air and struggled to think. I was sure, certain, positive it was, but what proof did I have? Vocalizations that could be speech? The waving and finger motions that might be words? Its strange desire to be with real people?

He went on, "You need to understand that how I would treat this thing depends greatly on what it is." I twitched my ears, agreeing. "You may be right, that this is no wild beast. It seems to bear some pieces of cloth or hide that is not its own. But is it a domestic beast, some strange pet? Or a person of type unknown?"

I coughed. I admit, I hesitated. Was there such a thing as a person not of our own type? There was still disagreement as to whether the Stick Men were people, and this did not look like them, except in superficial shape. Even the noises it made did not resemble the shouts I had heard. But I could not deny my heart. There were those tattered strips of cloth, which I hadn't even noticed. And I knew how any medic worth his oath would choose to help a domesticated beast in such extreme distress.

"It is a person," I whispered hoarsely.

"Are you sure?" I could only twitch my ears again, taut with anxiety. Could he gainsay my declaration?

"In that case, this person is incapacitated. Are you prepared to contract for its medical treatment? And to perform the duties of family in support of that care?"

At first, I could not quite absorb what he had said. I had to turn it over in my mind several times. And, well, at least there are some choices made easier by economic security. I wonder if, had I had known the outcome, I would have thought longer on the issue of performing family duties. There, memory cannot help, because present knowledge would have me decide exactly as I did, only more swiftly.

"Yes, sir. I so contract." I said at last. The doctor presented no arguments, but went straight to his work.

# 3

*"He repeatedly endangered the entire expedition. He slowed our progress and indulged in foolish diversions. His pedigree made the rest of the crew nervous. But he saved the mission. I saw that right away. So of course, I treated him like a real crewman."*

- Tereinse Alekwa
Expedition Leader

JEMENGA EXAMINED THE "PERSON" CLOSELY, touching it gently, but not moving it at all. He pulled tools from his medical bag and made measurements and recorded them. Then he crouched back on his haunches and hummed softly for a few moments, thinking. This close proximity the creature submitted to, or even eagerly accepted. Its wide, white-rimmed eyes watched the medic's face as intently as I did. At last, Jemenga seemed to come to some decision.

He placed his two great hands on each side of the creature's—person's—head, and wrapped his long fingers around its skull. Very gently, he lifted its head just enough to slip his fingers around the back, where it had lain in the muddy mulch all this time.

He closed his eyes, clearly concentrating on whatever information he was getting from his fingers. He probed carefully over the entire surface. The creature made a high, squeaky noise a few times, and the skin on its face grew wrinkled, so that its eyes grew narrow and nearly closed. But its color was stable and it held still, as if obedient to an order, at least to the extent that its continued tremors would allow.

The medic proceeded methodically. When finished with the head, he carefully lowered it down again and slithered his fingers down to the creature's thin, bony neck. Its eyes opened wide, and it squeaked again, but it held still. Surely, a fracture there would be very obvious.

"Yes," Jemenga said, as if in response, "I am looking for a structural failure. Even a minor crack could cause severe damage, as the main nerve bundle is in the spinal column, as it is for you and me. But here the spine is very strong; I would guess it's calciferous bone. No flaws detectable with simple touch or minor sonics, though the bones are jointed and I could be mistaking a break for a normal joint. I think we can risk moving her."

"Her?"

"Preliminary. Reasoning by analogy. Not important. There is a possible wound, but I need to get it into the open. Here, you can help." Under his direction, I helped him invert the creature, so that it was face-down. I had the unskilled-labor job of supporting its upper body and head so that its face was not in the muck.

Luckily for me, Jemenga worked swiftly. He removed a good deal of the hair covering on the back of the head. This had proved to be its own pelt and was quite thick. Then he squirted out a tube of cleanser and scrubbed the entire area. This elicited some noise from the patient. I wanted to twist down and look at its—her—face, as the creature seemed to possess the ability to spray water from her eyes … my arms were damp, but not near her mouth or nose.

At last, Jemenga grunted, "All right now. Turn her on one side, so she can breathe. Hand over that shirt of yours, so we can prop that head for a secure airway. And go on up and get the rest of the team. We'll need to camp here tonight. With luck, I can stabilize this wound by tomorrow."

I was not to be sent off so abruptly. "What wound?" I demanded. After all, I was going to pay for all this, and pay dearly, if his reputation was anything like what my aunts had claimed. But Jemenga was not at all reticent.

"Look here," he said, and I followed his direction to find a red oval cut into the skull, just at the point where it curved out to make room for the brain. It was a large wound to have in one's head, about the size of my grasping digits. "This may well have been the result of an attack of some kind, perhaps by those Stick Men who seemed to be pursuing her. It may be an old injury that abscessed ... became infected. But I don't see any obvious signs of infection. The one oddity is here," and he used his branched seventh digit to delicately point out three tiny wormlike growths or extrusions extending from the wound. "There is something familiar about those; it's something I read a long time ago. It just won't come to me now. I need time to think and look at this more closely. That research may have to wait until we return to civilization."

He sighed, stood, and stretched. "Either way, though, we should be ready to move on tomorrow. Go on now, boss-boy, fetch the others. I've got to pull out my archives and do some searching once I get this recorded and stitched up."

I hesitated as he turned away to rummage in his bag. There was something odd about that wound, about those strange threadlike extrusions. I leaned closer, and had to restrain my curious, unsterile fingers from investigating. I tasted the air, but could smell nothing but the bitterness of Jemenga's cleansing solution. Then, as I watched, one of the threads curled and straightened. A moment later, another twitched, and then a tremor swept through the creature's body from head to toe. And the third wormy growth vibrated so rapidly it blurred. Then all were still, though the person-of-unknown-type continued to tremble.

"Jemenga!" I said. "These white things here, they move, they—" But he cut me off brusquely.

"I know, I know. Be satisfied that you have interested me in this project. Go and explain to Alekwa how you have chosen to discard her schedule in favor of adopting a new family member." He waggled his fingers in my eyes and swatted me on the shoulder. And then he did laugh, a deep huffing in his chest, and I looked in his face. His eyes were sparkling, his ears pricked up, with the long guard fronds quivering excitedly. "Ha-hm," he chortled. "I had become so bored on this trip, I had forgotten why I came. This now, this is something worthy of Jemenga!"

So, it was with a light heart that I went to meet the wrath of Alekwa, who never hesitates to treat all team members as family.

That is, she regards all the members of an expedition as wayward children in desperate need of forceful, loud correction. I had been on my best behavior these past weeks, but now it was my turn to face that thunder.

I survived, though now I can confess that my ears were completely retracted by the time she was done, having absorbed lengthy and harsh descriptions of my ancestry and unfortunate descendants. My aunts had promised this would be an educational journey, and that afternoon my vocabulary was considerably broadened.

Nevertheless, by dusk we had pitched tents, cleared a firepit, and gathered wood. The penalty for my inconsideration was that not only was I required to draw my own mass in the campsite, but the extra requirements of Jemenga were my duty as well.

It had not occurred to my youthful mind that even a renowned medic does not work alone in the field. When he instructed me to "clean her up," I at first quailed at the idea, but it proved simple, even interesting. Jemenga kept up a continuous commentary into his recorder, and his observations helped me to think, as if at a distance from the task.

Shifting the patient to a safe work and study location called for four of us to lay hands on the creature. Making room in his chosen location—my much-mocked Luxury Executive brand tent—called for me to shift my own effects to the "gloriously healthy out-of-tent-doors." The minutiae of his work put me at his beck and call for the entire duration of our encampment.

The well-sealed tent made for a stuffy workroom, but Jemenga pronounced it sufficiently clean and draft-free for his requirements. I expected him to sew up that wound immediately, but instead Jemenga took a methodical approach. He insisted upon complete records, imaging the patient, her injuries, and other discoveries with the zeal of a peace officer documenting a crime.

Time and again, he pointed out my errors in perception. I was intrigued that the color of her hide was darker in many places; her back was a mottled pattern of blue and black and gold.

"Huh," Jemenga snorted, "Contusions."

I theorized on the loose folds of skin. Was it a defense mechanism? Did it provide extra layers of insulation? That earned a huff and a sigh.

"Dear innocent," he said quietly. "Starvation."

I fell silent then, focused on my work, thinking in my slow determined way. How could this be?

But my new mentor did not ridicule my foolish speculations; he focused entirely on his dual purpose of research and healing. "Find clothing. A blanket at the least."

I emptied my pack for the fine woolen shirt I'd been joshed into hiding at the start of the trek. Our patient seemed to appreciate its softness. I dared not go around pilfering anyone else's blanket, so turned over my own.

Through all this, my adoptee remained alert and stoic, reaching out to touch me whenever I was near, murmuring in that strange argot. *Haillyen imfrite ndwatshap. Haillyen howld mian. Haillyen tan keyu. Haillyen ware zazdyel.*

She did seem calmed by my presence, and I lingered, trying to puzzle out her meanings. After all, languages had been my most recent study at school. Ah, Turame! The deep amber eyes gazing into mine, the soft husky voice calling out declensions, the strong, elegant arms entwined with mine. Ah, well, that was either an age or a season ago; it was becoming difficult to keep track of the days.

Jemenga repeatedly put me back to work with a sharp "Ansegwe!"

"Ansegwe! Hold this light!"

"Ansegwe! Pick that up!"

"Ansegwe! Get me another card!"

I was heartened that the tremors seemed to have diminished, faded, but Jemenga did not seem to see this as such a useful indicator. "We do not have information enough to make a prognosis. We must record everything, collect all the data we can," he told me at every turn.

By the time the rest of the team had eaten, banked the fire, and rolled into their blankets, and even the patient appeared to have dozed off, Jemenga was fussing over preparations to, finally, close the wound he had so far only covered with a loose bandage.

"Ansegwe," he snapped, thrusting a capful of oily liquid at me, "Get her to drink this."

At least it was a new instruction, but I confess I was taken aback. "What is it?" I asked, bending my head to sniff the solution. It had a sweet scent, but with a bitter undertone.

"A sedative." At my blank look, he twitched his ears in annoyance. "Did you think I would sew a wound like that without anesthesia?"

There was a certain irony in waking the creature in order to send her to sleep. I touched her shoulder, but the doze seemed to have become slumber.

"Doctor Jemenga," I said. "She's already asleep, very asleep. Won't that do?"

"Ansegwe, do as I ask. Try sticking her with a needle, why don't you?"

That suggestion I chose not to follow. Instead, I gave her shoulder a little shake and tried one of the words she used so often, "Haillyen. Haillyen, wake up."

She groaned, a natural, ordinary sound, and turned her face to me, so the stained bandage was no longer in sight. But then she bared her teeth at me, which I am ashamed to say made me step back and turn to the medic.

"Jemenga … er …"

"Ansegwe."

I'm sure my swiveling would have been highly amusing. I was looking at Jemenga, but he was busy ignoring me for the moment. The speaker was behind me, but there was no one behind me but the creature. She simply held out her hand to me, that awkward angular gesture.

I looked back at Jemenga, and said, "What?"

"Ansegwe *kmere*."

It was the same hoarse, whispery voice I'd been listening to all afternoon. I could feel the spines on my back lifting, and it made me shiver. I whipped my head back around and stared at her. I think now that in that instant I had the confirmation that what I'd maintained all day was true. It was not entirely a comfortable sensation.

"Ansegwe," she said again.

# Ч

*"I tell you, it looked puny, but carrying it through the woods like that, it may as well have been a pregnant kazeran. I just kept thinking of the money. Kept wishing we'd wrung him for more. Can you believe I can make a living now, just on the interviews and autographs?"*

– Korton Alewere
Junior Mapping Engineer

THE CREATURE KNEW MY NAME. She said it again. "Ansegwe." She bent and unbent one long, bony finger, until I stretched out my smooth tentacular ones for her to hold. "*Sokay*," she said, softly, almost soothingly. "*Sokay*."

I hunkered down, looking into those small, flat eyes, wonderingly. With my free hand, I brushed myself on the chest. "Ansegwe, yes, I am Ansegwe."

I reached out and as softly as possible brushed my fingertips across the front of that high-fashion shirt of mine she was wearing.

"Do you have a name?"

For a moment, she was silent, and I was struck by a flash of imagination. What would it be like, my poorly-connected brain wondered, to find myself incapacitated, surrounded by a dozen skeletal wrinkly-skinned space invaders constantly talking blather? Would I have been able to pick out an individual's name from all the noise?

She seemed to study my fingers, running one of her rough ones along one of mine, feeling the junction of nerve and muscle fibers at the carpus joint. It tickled, and my fingers wriggled involuntarily. It was a bizarre sensation—disturbingly like, and yet very unlike, a normal joking tickle from a friend.

"*hoomeye hoomeye ndware ware,*" she said, and I couldn't tell if she were commenting on my anatomy or quoting poetry. "*hidno nymor azdyel isgon tuyo hiyegis himan haillyen. Haillyen.*"

"Haillyen?" I repeated. "Is that your name, then? Haillyen?"

Her response was a little puzzling. She bared her teeth again, though this time I was reasonably confident it was no threat. But then she made a rumbly gurgling noise that rose from down in her torso up to resonant chambers in her skull, so it seemed to both rise in pitch and grow louder. She only did it once, and then covered her mouth with one hand and patted mine with the other. I could tell by the curve of her face muscles that behind the hand she still was showing her teeth. Perhaps it was a gastric noise that was considered embarrassing. Or perhaps my pronunciation was offensive. But that was as close as I would ever come, as Jemenga interrupted our language lesson.

"Ansegwe, the sedative."

Without thinking at all, I simply handed the cup to the strange little creature … to Haillyen. She looked at it, poked that knobby, stuck-out nose over it and sniffed, and then simply drank it down. She didn't even make any untranslatable comments.

Something poked me in the shoulder. It was a stylus, with which Jemenga was jabbing me. He handed it to me, together with a dented and scratched old notepad.

"Now, while that takes effect, you take notes."

My dazed expression failed to satisfy. He frowned, wrapped my manipulative fingers around the stylus, and tapped the screen with it.

"Take notes," he said, slowly and deliberately. "Record your observations, which includes all these nonsense conversations. If you include conjectures, mark them as such."

I took this as a kind of challenge. Fortunately, my auditory memory is remarkably good.

When I looked up, the creature Haillyen was nodding drowsily. Jemenga, for his part, nodded contentedly. "A good initial estimate," he said.

I came to understand that he had had to make a measured guess on the quantity to administer. With my assistance, he dribbled a few more drams into his patient. We waited again, repeated the activity, and together watched her drop into a state of deep torpor.

There were a few inconveniences in turning over a sleep-soaked person rather than a cooperative one. Then improvisation was required to position the wound in a workable orientation with adequate light, while still ensuring the patient would continue to breathe.

And then I was required to be patient while Jemenga continued his detailed analysis of every step, insisting that, as my hands were free, I could record his brilliant insights. He stored more photographic images, while I was designated to note exactly what each image was meant to record. He tested the behavior of the strange wormy threads. (*The threads respond to touch individually and in concert,* I duly noted.) He timed tremor responses. My notes reflected my own assessment that these were no longer as severe as before.

Then Jemenga started a new line of inquiry—one which I found more difficult to manage. "Now for a little sampling," he said brightly.

Grasping a thin tubular instrument and humming to himself, Jemenga gently slid the end of the instrument deep into the wound. As for me, all four legs buckled simultaneously, and I slid gently to the ground.

"You play the role of family member too convincingly," Jemenga said drily, as I crouched there and tried to breathe the dizziness out of my head.

Perhaps simply taking notes would be sufficient. I did try that, but when his commentary turned to "infection of foreign ganglia" and "samples of alien brain tissue," my control of the stylus wavered.

"Doctor Jemenga, sir," I said unsteadily. "I believe it is high time I put some serious effort into reviewing my linguistic notes. Outside." And without waiting for him to either laugh or criticize, I staggered out into the cool night air.

I retracted my ears—to keep the wind out, I told myself—and concentrated on transcribing all the phonemic units I could recall accurately. Then I jotted down the sentences of our most recent exchanges, which I could still recall phoneme for phoneme. At last some real value could be gained from a skill I'd developed solely to avoid carrying note-taking equipment to class. I added a few illustrative sketches, endeavoring to see if I could form any initial impressions about grammar. Finally, I leaned against my pack to try to get more comfortable.

I had just settled down to a happy appreciation of the quiet forest night when bright, blazing light seared across my face. I sat up, blinked, and flicked my ears. Had someone lit a fire?

Well, if the great ball of the Sun counts as a fire, my guess was right. It was already morning. My back ached, my spines twitched with pinched nerves, and my mouth was dry, while my right-hand manipulatives ached with exhaustion. I clutched at vague streamers of a dream in which the spindly little alien had turned out to be my old sweetheart Turame's favorite linguistics professor—the one who was fond of screaming insults at students who failed to complete a syntax map to his perfectionist satisfaction. And in the dream, I had been presenting an extremely garbled map of the alien's own personal argot while being roundly castigated—in that gobbly tongue—for my ineptitude.

I woke feeling both foolish and incompetent. For a few seconds, listening to Alekwa shout orders, I muzzily wondered which character came from my imagination: the fussy professor or the talkative alien?

"Ansegwe! Get in here and cross-reference these samples!"

I sighed. Neither person was invented, and the screaming professor had been only a substitute for the demanding researcher. I rescued the little notepad from the leaf litter, scrabbled around to recover the precious stylus, and creaked to my feet. As my thoughts cleared, the thrill of adventure surged back, and I ducked into the tent, ready for anything.

It was a long day, but a good one. After Jemenga's comment on starvation, I was anxious to see if our strange new companion could benefit from our food. I arrived last to the breakfast queue, which meant my selection was limited to the least interesting plain vegetables; however, Jemenga allowed that these would likely be safe to offer her. Even so, he hovered alertly as she sampled small portions of each, swallowing each with a facial twist that I wished I could interpret properly. After each spoonful, she welcomed a drink of water from a bottle that Jemenga had rigged with tubing, like a baby's sipper-cup. She ate only a little before turning her face from the spoon.

"That's all right," Jemenga said, seeing concern glowing on my face. "She can't be feeling well after all the trauma yesterday. Give her time."

Nevertheless, after I put away the vegetable platter and the water bottle, she tried to sit up. It was a bit of a battle, but Jemenga managed to convince her to stay lying down. I settled down close by and pulled a meal bar from my bag to serve as my own breakfast. She perked up with interest.

"*hayyy* Ansegwe *gme kaanee*," she said.

"What? This?" I held up the horrid little nutrient bar and she reached for it. "Hmm." I said. "Those tiny teeth of yours are not up to these little chunks of rock-based cracker. Have you got grinding plates in your guts, too?"

She insisted, though admittedly I was assuming that using one finger to gesture repeatedly at a thing meant "Give me that!"

A little creativity seemed in order. After a thorough soaking in water, a chunk of hardtack became a mushy, cocoa-flavored pudding that, strangely enough, seemed to actually please her alien palate, as she gestured for more until the cupful of goo was empty. Then she tugged the spoon free of my hand and proceeded to clean it thoroughly with her weird pink tongue.

"Disgusting, but practical, I suppose," I said, retrieving the spoon and wrapping it in a reasonably-clean pocket cloth. "That's that, then. All the rest of my share of those abominable so-called ready-meals will be my gift to you."

Alekwa even permitted me to persuade a team of lower-level staffers to take it in turns to help me carry my new "family member" on the march. Need I mention that this involved payment?

Under Jemenga's guidance, I put together a makeshift litter that enabled a pair of us to trot along the trail with Haillyen (as I continued to call her) in between. That first morning, I took the lead position, thinking it more annoying (and therefore more expensive to delegate) to carry from behind. But she chattered loudly at me almost continuously, which had the combined effect of frustrating me and greatly amusing my comrades.

Oh, yes, I was already a laughingstock. It was difficult to miss the bawdy discussions going on amongst the crew, gauging the odds for success with my exotic mate. The continuous rumbling undertone of guffaws made me wish a few lightning bolts would slice down to justify all that thunder.

The sky cooperated with my wishes to the extent of clouding up, but that was all. At least that made the afternoon cooler. After the lunch break, I was sensible enough to move myself to the rear and let my helper lead. Haillyen could jabber to her heart's content, but she did not jabber quite so loudly. I continued to be frustrated, as I could not both take notes and carry my share of the weight, but on balance it was a better situation.

On the third shift, heading down to camp, I finally made my helpers do all the labor and tried to jot down notes and walk at the same time. This, of course, added to the general hilarity, as I did tend to walk into branches without ducking when I was looking down at the notepad. I began to wonder if I should be charging the other members of the expedition a special entertainment fee.

Once encamped, I again proved my worth by completing all the tasks assigned me by Alekwa and then carting water for and taking dictation from Jemenga. He was already well into a potentially award-winning treatise (according to him), and the physician was in such a good mood that he offered to include me as a secondary author. I quickly wrote myself in; at least my aunts would have something to show for those years of overpriced schooling.

Haillyen fell quiet in camp. There was much more to look at, and Jemenga gruffly allowed that it might be safe for her to sit up and watch the goings-on. When I had the leisure to sit while I worked at converting Jemenga's stream-of-thought dictation to a series of coherent paragraphs, I hunkered down next to our subject matter and tried to show her what I was doing. I expected the primitive to be at least interested in my magic box of words, but she only turned it over in her hands for a moment, bared her teeth, and handed it back.

"*Hipahd,*" she said. "*Nyss.*" Then she made a little sighing noise and leaned back. "*Hi yoozdta hevwuntu.*"

After composing another intricate paragraph of Doctor Jemenga Speaks, I had another idea. I cleared the little screen and carefully printed my name across it.

"Haillyen," I said.

She pushed herself up and wiped away more of that moisture that kept draining from her eyes. Was she evolved for a drier habitat?

I pointed at the screen. "Look. That's me, Ansegwe."

This time, she was less dismissive of my fabulous technological tool. She studied the screen thoughtfully. I was in agony to know if she understood the concept of writing or if she was just staring at an intriguing picture on the screen. So, I held out the stylus.

And she took it as if it were the most natural tool in the world, set it to the screen, and made her own scribble. Then she handed both items back and watched me in turn. It *looked* like writing. Was it phonetic? There were only four characters, though, and her name contained five or six phonemes.

I pointed with my little digits to each character, and experimentally sounded one possible combination: the balanced lever *Hai,* the fat round ball with a stem *l,* the drooping flower *ye.* But then there was another ball-with-stem. She responded with a high-pitched burbling noise and a flow of chatter, then snatched back the pad. Under that first word—which I gathered was not her name—she scratched out five new letters.

This set made more sense: two sticks leaning *Ha,* one tall stick *ee,* a short stick with a tiny speck floating above *l,* a fishhook with a large eye *ye,* and finally a stick with a quarter-loop attached *n.* She patted my carpus approvingly, then made a rubbing-out gesture on the screen. I showed her how to save and erase the screen, then thought some sense into myself and activated the main-memory lock. It wouldn't do to have her accidentally erase all my files.

But then she handed it back to me, gestured at the screen and said, "Ansegwe, Haillyen, *yoo riyat.*"

I wasn't sure if she wanted to see her own name or mine, so I wrote both and showed her which was which. And just as I thought I was getting somewhere, Jemenga popped out of his sanctum with a demand for humble labor … fetching water, what else?

When I finished, I went back to Haillyen. She was still fiddling with the notepad and was quick to show what she was up to. Her copy of my writing was awkward and childish, but very accurate.

"Well done," I told her. "I'm not sure I'd do as well with your letters."

She looked down and traced the letters in her name with one finger. *"Kess watt,"* she said thoughtfully, *"Hi kn riyat mi nayem hall bya miselv."*

# 5

*"I remember the performance Jemenga made Ansegwe put on, that one morning—when my brother and I both laughed so hard you would have thought an earthquake was happening. Somehow, though, watching the creature respond to their requests convinced us that maybe, just maybe, the tagalong gangster was right, after all."*

– Korton Tasegion
Senior Mapping Engineer

H AILLYEN STARED A WHILE LONGER at her successful writing exercise, tracing over the letters again with the stylus. A little more of the lubricating fluid in her eyes overflowed and dripped onto her hand, narrowly missing the notepad. She brushed away the moisture, slipped the stylus into its storage slot, and handed the tools back to me.

I settled myself a short distance away, unlocked the pad, and continued with my notes. I confess I was feeling more than a little full of myself: first person to make actual contact with an alien, first to hear alien language, first to read alien writing. The future, which had been nothing more than a tiresome return to the endless routine of upper-class education, was now packed with interest. I made as many plans as I made notes—some of those plans including a few intimate discussions of linguistics with the charming Turame. In the back of my mind, I composed indulgently romantic poetry and laughed at myself for doing so.

The next day, progress continued on an upward course. Jemenga was awake early, and so perforce was I. He had me fetch our three breakfasts from the front of the queue, as he had some project to try before we set out. He was fairly hopping with impatience by the time Haillyen finished working her way through her child-sized portion (a quantity by which, Alekwa curtly reminded me, the total supply was reduced, putting us all on shorter rations).

It seems that Jemenga had observed enough overall improvement over the previous day that he had decided to subject Haillyen to a battery of tests. The only amusing part of this project was his broad assumption that I would now be able to translate his instructions. My expert translation consisted primarily of miming the actions he desired: *Hold out one arm. Hold out both arms. Wiggle your fingers. Squeeze my hand.*

We shortly had a little audience of breakfasting explorers. Perhaps the first few onlookers were drawn by curiosity, to see what had finally earned Jemenga's interest. But the rest came to enjoy my performance, which apparently was the comedy hit of the season. More than one respectable person tipped his or her breakfast in the dirt in response to my memorable enactment of "raise both arms above your head." The rumbling of their laughter vibrated in my guts.

I was ready to practice some grinding-plate-resonating actions of my own, but Jemenga forestalled my lapse into combat mode. He had his own showstopper. Without even warning me, he grabbed Haillyen under the tops of her upper arms, and lifted her onto her feet. She stood, wobbling a little on those multi-jointed limbs.

"Ansegwe," called out one watcher. "Try doing 'move one foot then the other foot.' Maybe it'll chase you again!"

Jemenga snapped, "Shut up, you idiot." Typical Jemenga, then and now. And he didn't even waste time taking another breath before telling me, "Ansegwe, tell her to try walking."

Determined not to comply with the heckler, I tried simply gesturing to Haillyen to come towards me . . . and was relieved when she either correctly interpreted my come-hither finger-waggles or simply chose to try out her feet on her own. She tottered a few steps, unsteady, but under her own power and in control. I caught one arm to steady her and helped her turn and walk back to Jemenga. I could tell how pleased she was by watching that happy, horrendous snarl of hers growing wider moment by moment. I enjoyed some pleasure of my own from seeing the front row of the theater recoil when that fierce expression turned in their direction.

The show ended shortly thereafter. Haillyen tired quickly, and Jemenga insisted she return to resting. Oh, well, another day of toting, then about a half-day's march beyond the next camp before we would reach the pickup point. Fame and fortune were within sight, now.

The happy buzz in my ears helped shield me from the ongoing teasing comments chasing me along that morning. Ignoring those barbs, I worked out a forecast of the publicity the expedition would now earn for our investors. Hah. So much for all the naysayers who had predicted a negative cash flow that would bankrupt my aunts' company and shame the Family.

Then, Jemenga's scholarly paper would come out, with my name attached, and then, first the grant money and, eventually (of course), the Kalinidor Prize.

The closer we came to the end of the expedition, the more I realized how much I had gained, even beyond the excitement of the past couple of days. Roaming the wilderness, studying strange lands, plants, and animals, stood in perfect contrast to the sterility of abstract literary discourse and business revenue analysis. Neither literature nor business appealed to me at all anymore. Too bad for the family who'd invested in that education.

*Hah!* I told myself. *It's their own fault for insisting on sending an unemployable gadabout to monitor this trip in the first place.*

At the first break, Haillyen tried a few more steps, and even demanded the luxury of a few private moments in the bushes. At the second break, though, she seemed more wobbly, not less, and sat down almost immediately. Her speech seemed odd, too. The words I had started to recognize, though by no means interpret, sounded blurred, as if I was listening through water. I decided it was not my tired ears and overactive imagination when she complained.

"Han's'we," she mumbled. "*P'o'lm.*"

Haillyen gestured with her left hand up and down her right side. She seemed to be having some difficulty moving her right arm, and poked and rubbed it as if the nerves were asleep.

Something from those irritating first-aid classes jangled an alarm bell in the back of my mind. Haillyen shook her head and rubbed her good hand across her eyes as if trying to clear her vision. I ran for Jemenga.

From there, the day went downhill.

Yes, he agreed, it was a stroke. He called it a "Cerebral Vascular Event" and continued, more to himself than to me, "It has to be bleeding. Pressure on the supply vessels from a hematoma." Yet I caught the faintest hint of wavering as his fingertips formed the words. "Not a clot, no. Couldn't be. I should have put in a drain."

Alekwa objected fiercely to a hold in the march. We were carrying the weird creature, anyway, she pointed out. And continuing would only bring us closer to better medical equipment. My opinion was not called for, but Jemenga's was well-heard.

"We are not moving one fingerbreadth before I get this hematoma drained. I need tubing. Sterile." And he was already unpacking his bag, searching for something to serve his purpose. For one instant, he turned his glare on me and barked, "Ansegwe! Go get water. Now."

There are some advantages to being obsessed with order and efficiency. By the time I returned, Jemenga was already re-stitching the wound, this time with a red tube projecting from the web of fine stitchery with which the wound was held closed. I bent in curiously, but he pressed me back.

"No time for fainting, schoolboy," he said gruffly. And he dumped out the water and handed me the dripping pail. "Time to run."

The rest of the team was already moving out and I was hefting my end of the litter before I realized that the tube itself was clear, not red. Yes, Haillyen's blood was red, not aquamarine, and that fluid oozed slowly through the tube, dripping gently onto the leaf litter below.

Still, I had no trouble with keeping up a strong pace. Haillyen's chatter was conspicuously absent. Every time I would think she had lapsed into unconsciousness, those thick eyelids would flutter open and she would make some feeble imitation of her vigorous gestures, mutter some garbled phrase, or—even worse—produce a lopsided version of that happy snarl. Jemenga trotted alongside, tapping on his hand console at the same time.

Proving agile as well as brilliant, he easily avoided crashing into any trees despite the density of vegetation on the woodland trail.

The next six hours were terrible, but at least I was useful. Every step I took carried us one step closer to home—and help. Jemenga kept me busy, emphasizing to me that he was relying on my status reports to gauge if and when to administer more medication. As long as Haillyen kept talking, I listened to her and made it obvious I was listening. When she fell silent, I filled the gap myself, with words meant to encourage, despite the sure knowledge that the words themselves meant nothing.

Jemenga insisted it was not as bad as it seemed, that the drain appeared to have been successful. But each of my reports to him described less responsiveness, less coherence, less strength in the affected side. Worse, though I expected Haillyen to fall into unconsciousness, she remained awake the entire time, painfully conscious of increasing debilitation. When she stopped talking, I burned to know if she had simply grown frustrated with the physical effort, or if the stroke were stealing the words themselves from her. Would I ever learn the meaning of that fascinating jabber?

We made good time. Alekwa generally set a steady pace meant for high endurance. On that final leg, she led us at speeds more representative of footraces than wilderness strolls. The last two hours were brutal: a pounding scramble down the zig-zag trail from the upper hills we had been exploring to the valley floor where cool river water flowed from a wide, glimmering lake. We all waded in to bathe our agonized feet. At the bottom of the trail, we were permitted ten minutes of total collapse—which for me meant exchanging notes with Jemenga while stretched out on the ground rather than while jogging through the woods.

The brief rest was surprisingly invigorating, no doubt due to the stimulating effect of the proximity of our endpoint. The dash along the river to the transfer point was easy, just an afternoon trot with the family. From a half-mile off, we could hear the hum of machinery, and we all hurried faster towards the gateway home. A word from Jemenga, and the four of us were rushed to the head of the queue. Jemenga swept ahead, barking orders even as we trotted under the glowing arch of the Translation Device, with Ensargen and I maneuvering Haillyen's stretcher between us. This time, I hardly even noticed the headaches and disorientation endowed by the shift between Deep Valley World and home.

Then, to my lasting consternation, it was as if the translation process had channeled me to an even more bizarre universe—let us call it Medical Establishment World. In moments, Haillyen had been extracted from my presence, whisked away I knew not where. Ensargen stepped back, flickered his fingers at me in a silent *"I'm off. Good luck, kid."* and dodged around the incoming officials to find his own way home.

My taskmaster, friend, and teacher transformed himself into that most foreign of beings, the Skilled Physician, and Jemenga descended into the mysterious company of other S.P.'s, their voices and fingers fluently exchanging the arcane language of advanced medicine. I followed them out of the maze of the TransComm complex, where they piled into an official-looking van and rolled away, still gesturing to each other.

As for me, I commandeered the next vehicle that rolled up and abused the privilege of my family name to demand the driver follow the van full of doctors three miles to the nearest hospital. A kindly, roly-poly nurse greeted me at the hospital entrance with warm words and a calming hand on my arm, then ushered me to the sterile, tree-less environment of an interior cubicle lit by a single flickering fluorescent tube. There, a dull-eyed hospital administrator with no medical expertise whatsoever presented me with an immense stack of hard-copy paperwork and the admonition to complete all of it *immediately.*

# 6

*"We put the boy on the team to remind the others of the stakes in that venture. But as the family motto reminds us: Every Action Has Profit. Who imagined what form our profits would take?"*

– Varayla Ansele
CFO, Varayla Industries

MY AUNTS TELL ME I DID WELL, that the demands of an arcane, secretive bureaucracy can wear down even a person of great personal strength. I think they were pleased to see me subjected to this torture; it has always enlivened the old ladies to watch me suffer through one of life's transitional experiences. And I must grudgingly admit that I learned the system well; that investment has paid out compounded returns many times as I've had to cope with the Medical Establishment for other purposes over the years.

But at the time, I was young, idealistic, and impatient. It was inconceivable that treatment would be deferred until paperwork was complete. It was incomprehensible that care would be restricted without assurance of financial resources. It was unbelievable that I was denied access to my official, documented, contracted adoptee Family Member "for security reasons."

"What security reasons?" I rumbled at the District Peace Officer blocking entrance to what had been an outpatient clinic but now served as an Isolation Unit, according to the hand-lettered sign taped to the sealed door. "What are you afraid of? Invading hordes of comatose invalids? Radical political movements based on alien government structures? What pointless fears are they feeding you goons?"

It did not improve my demeanor at all to have several of the DPO's comrades haul me away forcibly. It was by no means helpful to receive a ten-minute lecture delivered by the local Peace Officer on how I ought to have been charged with uncounted violations, from Insulting a Representative of Peace to Damaging Hospital Property.

I could not bring myself to mimic anything like remorse, but the fat balance on my personal account served to soothe the soul of the hospital's Chief Administrator. That good lady had wanted me imprisoned for smashing a cartload of pre-prepared patient meals against a wall. It's just possible that the Peace Officer stole a peek at my account links and drew his own conclusions on the political ramifications of hurling me into the local dungeon. Thus was I spared, set loose to offend more Free Individuals.

Instead, I chose to exercise an incredible degree of self-restraint and filed my requests through proper channels. Given that I was behaving myself, my own dear old ladies quietly applied their particular variety of specific impulse to speed my demands' trajectory through the system.

It was a good thing, too, because as soon as information began to percolate through the various screens the Medical Establishment used, the Government was on my case. However, by then I had in hand all the required identity cards, relationship documents, and contractual support agreements appropriate to any immigrant sponsored by a family member. Hah. Make that "sponsored by a Family Varayla member."

The bleary-eyed bureaucrat assigned to process my brand-new paperwork at the Citizen Registry saw her opportunity immediately. Rather than a cartload of deportation orders, appeals, contradictions, and grotesque public and sequestered testimony, she could choose the five-second, three-form process of issuing an instant visa, a naturalization-in-progress authorization, and a passport citing my guardianship.

I'd lived a sheltered life, true, but now I was deep in the thick of all that business I had been sheltered from.

Perhaps I need to explain. I have hedged a bit about Varaylas Adeleke and Ansele. They are the respectable members of the Family, but respect for any portion of my extended family derives more from the power and influence wielded by its members as a class than from the innate goodness of any individual.

For instance, consider that I was raised by my aunts, from quite a young age. Did you think it a cultural feature of my people, that parents defer childrearing to their siblings? Or did you think in passing that some tragedy must have overcome my parents?

Well, you might call it tragic, as the ends derived from the faults of the individuals. My parents were sentenced to a decade housed in separate off-shore penal institutions, after a complex tower of graft and influence peddling collapsed during an unexpected shift in the capital markets. Using their own methods to, shall we say, obtain an unscheduled release from custody, they failed to adjust their vocational impulses. Consequences accrued.

They were stupid not to have seen disaster coming. They were dishonest to have engaged in those activities in the first place. And they were ruthless about cutting their losses when trouble began to close in on them.

It was easy to learn about the situation. It was in all the newscasts at the time; even at my tender age it was obvious that Mummy and Daddy had done Very Bad Things. I was correspondingly angry with them. It was their fault I was alone—an only child. It was their fault I had to go live with those boring old ladies who were obsessed with school and wouldn't let me spend my money as I liked. If I felt like smashing things once in a while (or several times a day), well, It Was Their Fault. A significant portion of my inheritance money was expended on the services of practitioners of the vague science of psychology.

That whole business, the Collapse of TelComm, ended up in the textbooks, as an example of criminal bungling and its consequences. The Varayla Family was deeply embarrassed, expressed tremendous public remorse, and spent millions in compensation. And, of course, the family Syndicate tightened its organization to prevent further such debacles.

The Family even spun off a series of truly above-board companies to shield from view their more traditional, but less attractive, activities. Ansele and Adeleke snatched up the best of these: the company that owns and operates the powersats that beam down the energy that keeps the economies of the developed world booming. It was an easy pick for "privatization," as no one in the Family wanted outsiders getting the idea that the world's most well-known gangsters had the power to blast downside cities with microwave radiation.

The ladies had their smarts; they could have fallen under suspicion because of their closeness to Daddy. Now they were in the clear, managing a strictly regulated, heavily inspected firm with representatives from seven major governments constantly tramping through their files and facilities. Even so, the profits were better than most of the illicit enterprises that had established the Family's fortunes back in the rough-and-tumble days of the Consolidation.

My beloved aunties' investment in TransComm was not just a business venture.

Insinuating themselves into the internationally-funded Transfer Project played into their political machinations; the old ladies' most active hobby was buying up politicians. After only twenty years, they had already reached the upper echelons of the home government, and had positive ties in five of the other six regional governments. Aunt Adeleke had also observed that Translation Device technology—and its inevitable spin-offs—would open up new worlds for all the Family's businesses. As for Aunt Ansele, she once confided to me that she found the fantastic notion of instant transportation to an alien universe purely appealing for its own sake. It is no more than a myth that laypersons lack an appreciation of science-for-its-own-sake.

As trustees of my holdings, the aunts had made it clear that my cash flow would be cut off if I failed to develop a career track. Going on the expedition had been presented as a qualifying activity. They hardly expected what I would come back with. But I have to give my aunts their due: upon my return, with a new and surpassingly strange affiliate, they never hesitated to back me. After all, we were Family.

The hospital months were, though I hate to admit it, fascinating times. I learned more about medicine and law than I had ever expected to learn in my lifetime.

At first, the physicians seemed not at all focused on helping Haillyen. First, they did nothing. Then they did even more nothing. Through trial and error, I developed a form of ranting that generated answers. Not that the answers were satisfying. The patient was stable. More data was needed. They were gathering data. More experts were being flown in.

The data gathering involved scans. By the end of that, I was acquainted with every established and experimental method for acquiring information about the interior workings of an organism, short of dissecting it. They fired sound, high-frequency electromagnetic radiation, and magnetic beams through her body. They made photographic images, moving pictures, three-dimensional layered digital scans, chromatographs of bodily fluids, and chromosome charts of genetic material.

In no time, the study team was huge. There were biologists, geneticists, neurologists, and chemists. I began to think of them all as The Ists. The Ists were in my way when I wanted to check on my Family Member. The Ists had to be forcibly reminded to acquire my permission before trying out one of their blasted procedures. The Ists were always reluctant to have me present, protective of their precious medical secrets. They trained me well in the means of determined resistance that have stood me in good stead to this day.

In the back of my mind, I had this notion the investigators would happily disassemble Haillyen if I wasn't keeping an eye on things. But I never brought that idea to the forefront.

Neither did I attend to the recurrent images of those strange wriggling fibers, the never-explained wound, Jemenga's voice on the recorder … *alien neural tissue intrusions*. And I could never bring myself to ask, as if asking invited in far too many possibilities.

Finally, I put my feet down, and demanded treatment. It shouldn't be so hard to make a few guesses, I told them. (I believe that statement was delivered at a very high decibel level, but that was all. Contrary to anything you may have heard, I did not threaten to strike anyone. I nobly refrained from even hinting that I did have the connections necessary to arrange for permanent changes in the local population of bureaucrats and Ists, including their immediate families and close friends.)

At this point, I gained an insider's education concerning the medical subsystem termed Physical Rehabilitation, known to its unfortunate denizens as Rehabi. The name evokes images of coming home. It sounds so serene, as if it involves a series of calming strolls in tamed parklands. But Rehabi is in fact a highly refined system of torture, implemented in such a way as to encourage the participants to do everything in their power to escape. The only escape is the release form signed by the patient's assigned Skilled Physician. That signature is forthcoming only if particular milestones are met. Achieving those milestones involves both pain and frustration, not to mention mind-numbing repetition of both elements.

Yes, I would guess that you must have heard of a system such as this. But have you ever endured its embrace? Accompanied a person who will require significant assistance? After our very first session, in which it was demonstrated for me just how physically incompetent Haillyen was, I had to leave the building. I was desperate. I had to run three times around the "parklike setting" before my flight responses settled to mere muscle quivers. It was shameful, but better than collapsing into the gibbering horrors in front of the medical staff.

Was this to be my lot? Pushing food into that flat, colorless face? Managing transit times to be sure wastes were disposed of properly? Exercising fingers, arms, and legs? Dressing? Bathing?

And hoping, of course, and talking. The running lecture stressed and restressed the importance of carrying on active, if one-sided, conversation. So much for leisurely literary luncheons with over-educated young ladies. So much for late nights at the racetrack.

I had my determination to fall back on. No one was going to call me a shirker. No one was going to point at my family name to explain away my own incompetence. So what if I never went to parties? So what if my gambling expenses took a nose dive?

I attended every single rehabilitation session. It got better— or at least bearable. I learned to be efficient, but also to push for Haillyen to do it for herself. I learned that watching pain hurts. I learned to take in stride activities that had sent me out running in the early days. And there was progress. Milestones were met.

One morning, Jemenga came to visit along with a hospital staffer I hadn't seen before. A youngish staffer, clean-lined, dark-toned, with finely-turned legs. Not that I noticed.

"This is Kateseo," he said. "Haillyen is being released today."

"Huh?" (True, in those days it seemed my new life had forced me to abandon my often-mocked verbosity. Yes, yes, so tragic that I lost the art of poetic speech, never again to regain it.)

"It's time for you to take her home, Ansegwe."

# 7

*"If you had told me, five years ago, that the kindest, most effective caregiver I'd ever work for would be some diamond-assed playboy, I'd've told you to go for a long swim in a dry hole."*

– Kishada Tumbal
P.A.

JEMENGA RUMBLED IMPATIENTLY, but Kateseo, that pretty young administrator, laid a shapely hand across my arm and repeated herself, "Ansegwe, are you listening? It's time for you to take her home."

"Home? Today? Already?" As the information began to crystallize in my mind, the anxiety I thought belonged in the past came oozing back. "No. We're not ready."

I mentally ran over Haillyen's capabilities. She could eat, sort of, but still needed assistance. She still could not speak. She could walk, but needed support. She could not dress herself. And there was still the mystery of that original injury, the twitching wormlike enigmas.

*Focus on today*, I told myself, echoing the highest law in the world of Rehabi.

Kateseo gestured to the doorway. "Shall we walk?" she said. "I find it helps the discussion."

I had been about to shove my way past the pair of them; on balance it was more politic to accept her invitation. However, I'm afraid my anxiety established a difficult pace; Kateseo was elegantly petite, so she had to conduct her portion of the discussion at a trot.

To my surprise, the topic of discussion was not Haillyen, but myself. It was entirely usual, I was informed, for caretakers to feel both overwhelmed and excessively dutiful. There were natural consequences, from nonproductive anxiety (as displayed during our talk) to severe depression. There was help available. I should not hesitate to seek such help. There was no stigma attached. I must feel responsible for my own well-being as well.

Anger is a workable antidote to anxiety. My need to stride out the jitters metamorphosed into a desire to strike out at this pusillanimous busybody, regardless of her otherwise fine attributes. I was perfectly well; there was nothing wrong with *me*. Haillyen needed help—she needed *my* help; I was conspicuously able-bodied and coherent.

Indeed. I was coherent to any listener within a quarter mile. Meanwhile, Kateseo withstood my tirade with nothing more than a calm, even bored, expression, her ears politely extended. Then she handed me a brightly-colored folder and walked away, calm as a midsummer day.

I marched to the nearest waste bin, but at the last second hesitated, and opened the folder.

There were little brochures on recognizing and coping with a disgusting array of neural dysfunctions. There were references to support associations for each named mental problem. One by one, these bits of rubbish were relegated to the trash.

But then I came upon the List of Practical Nurses. That one I pulled out, studied thoughtfully, and saved. At last I had found a type of help I could accept. And there was a list of books. Books are always quiet, reassuring, and private. Those, too, I could bring on board. But the rest of Kateseo's packet was relegated to reprocessing. Soon enough, those fibers would emerge from some factory, ready to be turned into new booklets, in order to be therapeutically discarded by some other person in distress.

So. We went home. Despite the unrelenting chores, there was something inexpressibly easier about being at home together. For "home," I must clarify, I should write "aunties' cottage in the country."

This was the place I had spent most of my growing-up years—at least the time I wasn't trapped at school. The estate was small and therefore manageable. It had a quiet, private garden that ran down a slope behind the house, gradually becoming less of a garden and more of a wilderness until a cold, rushing stream cut through the property and declared the area officially wild.

On our arrival, I could not help but gallop downslope and splash my feet in the stream, as I had done on every previous arrival. Haillyen waited stoically, arranged in a seemingly relaxed pose in the resting chair that Jemenga had had specially designed for her. On my return, I looked eagerly into her face for some response, amusement at my antics perhaps. But her colors did not vary, so if there was emotion expressed, it was not understandable to me.

"Well, my dear Family Member," I said, shaking off the eerie feeling that I was speaking to a silent ghost. "Are you hungry? Let us retire to the kitchen for our meal."

I chose only a simple stew of grains and vegetables, but the fresh hot food soothed away not only the day's travel, but also the weeks of reconstituted compost and hospital dining. As I spooned Haillyen's share, I reminisced about our days with the Expedition.

"Remember how Alekwa complained about your drain on our resources? And the time half the team dropped their breakfasts in the dirt?" Strange, how even those embarrassing moments came back to me in bright, attractive colors. Finally, I had to put down the spoon and pick up a napkin to dab away the lubricating fluid that still, so often, overflowed from her eyes.

Deep in the night, engulfed in the quiet that I had so longed for, I woke trembling. The dream was so startlingly clear in my mind. It seemed more like memory than nightmare. Not groggy in the least, but staggering with one pressure-numbed leg, I stumbled down the hall and peered around the corner into Aunt Adeleke's room.

Haillyen was the picture of peaceful repose. She was rolled up like a caterpillar in a bundle of blankets. I stood for some time, letting the reality overwrite the dream. There were no strangulating cords of quivering alien brain tissue roping about the room. Only the barely-perceptible wavering of the low-level fluorescent night-lights. Finally, worried she might wake and catch me staring, I crept back to my own sleeping mat. It was a relief when the sun finally appeared.

Luckily, such nights were few. But that first afternoon set the pattern for many days to follow. The Practical Nurses came and went, shift on shift. The Physical Adaptors appeared on their own rigid schedule, performed their ritualistic exercises, and vanished down the road.

Twice a week, every four days without fail, the grocer's boy arrived leading my old childhood favorite, the kazeran Erekulu, who still pulled the high-wheeled cart loaded with groceries and books. And, while the boy unloaded the goods and loaded up the rubbish, I would wheel out Haillyen's chair. Then the kindly beast would snuffle in her upturned hands for treats while I rubbed his favorite itchy spots and whispered in his tiny ears.

"When I was little," I told Haillyen. "I could actually ride on Erekulu's back, if you imagine that. Aunt Ansele had a joke, which I don't remember very well. It went, 'What has eight legs, two arms, and half a brain?' Can't guess it? 'A silly ass on a brainless donkey!'

"It made everyone laugh. But, you know, I don't really think he's brainless. You and I now know many people in the government who are much less intelligent."

Indeed, the animal seemed to have a way of knowing just how far he could go with Haillyen. Where he would bump my shoulders to demand attention and then nibble at my fingers, Erekulu was a perfect gentleman with her, scooping up the treats I'd planted with the gentlest brush of his soft, snaky tongue, tucking his nose in the shelter of her stringy head fur and tasting her scent reassuringly.

In between those visits, I would cook, we would eat, and I would read the books and write out a list for the next round. The days were full. I read assiduously, but still felt that my progress was slow. There were so many interruptions built into my schedule. The exercises had to be performed three times daily, and I painstakingly followed the current week's variation on the instruction sheet. Haillyen had to rest at prescribed times, and she had to walk every afternoon.

Jemenga came regularly, every other week or so. He was always jovial, wrapping his long black arms around me, praising Haillyen's progress. It made me grey a little in shame, for I knew he was shading the truth to cheer me up.

And every time, I would start to ask him if his team of experts had ever come to any conclusions about the weird dangling fibers. Sometimes, my memory described them as wires, sometimes as worms, sometimes as sentient brain-sucking monsters. I wanted to know if I should be relieved, worried, anxious, or afraid.

Instead, I would fuss over meal preparations, tidying, or helping Haillyen with some mindless but necessary task. Jemenga would press me to make the practical nurses do more of the work, and I would grumble that they were good for the distasteful jobs, but certain things they seemed unable to do properly.

"Ansegwe!" he said, on more than one such occasion. "They are professionals, you must trust their skill!"

"Bah," was my response. "They will make her eat food she doesn't like. They will take her for 'walks' in front of the video, because it is too hot for them outside and they might miss a good episode. They are too rough with her during exercises; they are too used to our kind of people. And some of them do not treat her like a person at all."

This was a sore point with me, and it struck to the center of my current reading frenzy. I was studying everything I could find on the subject of personhood—of sentience and consciousness.

The physicians were nearly unanimous that, in people, stroke and other brain ailments can leave a person unable to communicate, yet aware of his or her surroundings. My reading had led me to their evidence: numerous stories of recovered persons who reported in detail their experiences while uncommunicative. I had also found plenty of reports of people who never did recover from a severe multilateral stroke. When I read one of these, it would trigger several days of grumpy obsessiveness.

The more esoteric texts I consulted stretched my reading comprehension skills to their limits. It seemed there was an entire field of study devoted to the question of what constitutes a sentient being—a real person. To some of these cold-hearted bastards, any person as afflicted as Haillyen should be demoted automatically to non-person, as communication is the center of their definition.

I was a little more comfortable with the class of philosopher who defined sentience on the basis of self-awareness. Does a kazeran know himself when he sees his reflection in a watering trough? With a person such as Haillyen, her sentience before the stroke was obvious; afterwards, it was at least impossible to disprove.

I even experimented. I brought her a mirror and tried to gauge her reaction.

"Look here, Haillyen, what do you think?"

She was neither fascinated nor disturbed by what she saw. I confess I had been hoping for a dramatic response, some version of *Look, there I am!* I swear she looked, that her eyes met her own and then mine in our shared reflection. But it was only a moment before she turned away, making those soft, short inhalations I'd learned to associate with melancholy days. I left the mirror as it was, propped carefully on the bureau. At the very least, its reflections of light from the window would brighten her room.

# 8

*"Initially, I believed the request to be a prank. Indeed, until the draft of the first paper landed on my desk, I still harbored doubts. The boy's reputation—let alone that of his relatives—was not consistent with a desire for reading esoteric texts and generating more of the same."*

– Tsulander Tkonle
Professor, Philosopher, Talk Show Favorite

THE MIRROR EXPERIMENT had to be set aside for the moment, in favor of mechanical repairs. I ended up spending much of the rest of that day with my fingers tangled in the innards of the humidification system I'd had installed. I'd been so pleased with the system at first; Haillyen's eye drainage had gradually diminished over time. I no longer carried around those annoying scraps of cloth. But that day, the drainage had returned full force and now the problem even seemed to affect Haillyen's respiratory system. She would gasp and seem to be choking, and then breathe rapidly, with a high squeaky sound. It was incredibly alarming, though the nurse on duty at the time insisted that all measurable systems were normal for the patient and no bacterial or viral agents were in evidence.

Jemenga answered my frantic call with forbearance and promised to drive out later that day, but if her condition worsened, he reminded, my call should be to emergency services.

Fortunately, my tinkering seemed to work at last. Haillyen's alarming symptoms abated over a few hours, and by evening Jemenga was able to devote his visit to reciting his usual exclamations of "What wonderful progress you are making here!"

•          •          •

The next shock I was to endure came on the very next visit of my favorite among the various Physical Adaptors. At the end of his session, Tumbal tapped on the kitchen door and cheerfully pronounced that Haillyen had completed her therapy work, and that this would be last time we would see him. While I stood at the kitchen table, stunned, with a half-eaten bowl of soup in front of me and the spoon dripping in my hand, he thumped a fat folder onto the counter and congratulated me.

"It has been a pleasure working with you, sir," he continued, suddenly all formal with leave-taking protocols. "Rarely have I had the good fortune to have such diligent support from a patient's family. It is entirely to your credit that she has reached this high level of accomplishment."

I was thrown back to my state of the day Haillyen had been discharged from the hospital. "What? But she hasn't recovered!"

He shifted back a little on his haunches, seeming to consider the tell-tale color shifts in my face. I had an urge to ask his professional assessment of my emotional state. I wasn't sure if what I was feeling was anger, fear, or sadness.

"Mr. Varayla—" he began.

"Ansegwe," I snapped. He paled just slightly, and I recognized a twinge of guilt in my mixed-up feelings.

"Sir," he temporized. "Think back. When you arrived home, she could not feed herself, clothe herself, walk unaided. She now does all these tasks. Perhaps her performance is not up to your standards, but improvement in the smoothness of motor skills occurs gradually, and that progress is now under her own control. With your continued encouragement and moral support, rest assured you will see continued gains."

I couldn't help myself. I knew he was being reasonable, comforting, and more verbose that he'd been all year. But my left hand just curled up to the carpus and slammed the table. My soup sloshed out of the bowl, and I only felt more anger at the future annoyance of having to clean up the mess. I uncurled my legs to stand to my full height, leaned over the table to put my roiling face right up to his, and roared, "But she still can't talk!"

The Physical Adaptor's deep orange had paled to nearly yellow, but he stood his ground.

He even had the temerity to loop one of his powerful arms over to grasp my shoulder. He pinched just slightly, enough to give me a little shake, which reminded me of the strength required of a person whose daily work involves manipulating the muscles of adults of all sizes.

Yet his answer was gentle, and surprising. "Sir, it's not that she's not talking to you. It's that you aren't listening."

He disengaged and started to turn away. I was grateful for that, certain that I was practically pink with confusion and embarrassment.

"Wait," he said, talking to himself more than to me. And he twisted to snag a pen from the satchel on his back. "Look here, I've seen what you've been reading. You're going a bit far afield in my opinion. Here are a couple of references that might put you back on track." And he scribbled down a few titles, and an author's name. "Good luck, sir." And he was closing the front door, with his characteristic care and quiet, before I had gathered even a simple Thank You.

So, being Ansegwe, I thundered through the back door and around the side of the house, to intercept him at his car.

"So sorry," I panted. "You've been a great help, Tumbal. If there's ever anything I can do for you, just ask."

His color rushed back, and we touched fingers properly this time. I ventured a laugh, hoping my behavior would be filed under *'everybody knows Ansegwe just has this temper'*.

Hastily, then, I added, "Just, you know, it's got to be the legal stuff. We're supposed to be good guys nowadays."

He laughed then, too, and we embraced. I waited while he squeezed into his tiny car. As it whirred off down the road, I felt a modest thrill of pride at the realization that my aunts' business was indeed good-guy stuff, for, without the electric power to run that car of his, I'd have either been on my own in the peaceful country house or trapped in the city, arms tangling with strangers every day.

When the dust was settling back on the road again, I turned back to the house. Haillyen was there in the kitchen, perched on her own odd little chair. She stood up when I came in. The binder lay where Tumbal had plunked it down, but the piece of paper with the list was gone. I cast about for it, under the table, inside the binder, but it had disappeared.

I picked up a cloth and made a half-hearted stab at wiping up the spilled soup. But my mind was not on the job, and I ended up crouched back at my place, doodling in the damp smear with one manipulative.

Then suddenly, there was a hand on mine, lifting it up, and the cloth reappeared, wiping the mess clean this time. When I looked up, Haillyen stopped cleaning and stood staring at me with those shiny little eyes blinking and blinking. She reached out one bony hand and gave my shoulder a little tug, oddly reminiscent of Tumbal's wake-up gesture.

"What do you want?" I asked, frustrated.

And she handed me the piece of paper. It could have been blown to the floor when I swept by in my rush. She must have heard my departure, followed the furious sounds, and found the list on the floor.

I looked down at the paper. Tumbal was right; these I had not read. Even the authors were unfamiliar—at least one was foreign. However, Tumbal's handwriting, unlike mine, was easy to read:

*Essentials of Nonverbal Communication, by Asvelan Kulumbu*

*The Language of the Forest, by Palawan Vejr*

*Who's Talking Now? by Trjia Qwijlian*

*and look for anything by Tsulander Tkonle*

I looked up at Haillyen and waved a little smile with my soupy manipulatives. She bared her teeth at me. My pulse picked up, and I could feel my color coming back.

"Thank you," I said.

•    •    •

Still, for the longest time, there was no change. In retrospect, it was the easiest stretch. My own tasks were not too difficult. I let go the practical nurses. My aunts remained feverishly anxious to get me established in a self-supporting career, but I self-righteously cited Family Duties and went back to school.

Well, it was school by remote. Tumbal's list only got me started. As he hadn't actually given me any titles for T. Tkonle, I simply had the Family machine track the fellow down and established a direct communication.

Luckily for me, Tkonle was a professor at Korlo University. His works were mainly thick, scholarly things . . . but spiced with a humor exactly to my taste. He had published two money-making tomes in popular style, with which he was pleased to tell me he had supported a goodly stream of students. I wondered if he might be interested in taking on a student of independent means. Would it be feasible for such a student to work via telecom and correspondence? Would it help if that student had a communication project in progress?

So, in short order, I was a Scholar-in-Training, with a duly appointed Mentor, a research project identified, and the most traditional component firmly in place—a family in despair at the thought that the presumed heir displayed no interest in Profitable Enterprise.

Oh, but like most business-oriented families, my aunts were simply ignorant of the business of research. Tkonle was a prominent person—a Scholar in great demand by students. Students needed support, materials, tuition fees, and transport to conferences to present their papers—shall we say ... to deliver their products. Like any captain of industry, Tkonle had a stunning mastery of developing just enough interest in his proposals to extract from sponsors the maximum possible investment, and he knew how to parlay that investment to maximum productivity.

Almost against my will, I readily absorbed his techniques in that arena. As I cranked out my first contribution to his list of publications, I ruefully reflected that my aunts could not have sought better training for a future CEO than the process of obtaining grants. In research, as in business, money begets money.

On the day after my (and Tkonle's) paper, "Non-Universality of Color-Based Communication," passed review muster and reached the massive audience of the Union of Communication Research, Jemenga appeared at my door with his copy of our half-written paper on those first-contact adventures during the Expedition.

"I must have this finished. Yesterday," he insisted, waving away the hot drink I was offering him. "They've finally declassified the information. I must be first." I paused with a cup halfway to my own mouth.

"Declassified?"

"Yes, yes, of course we could not publish our work so long as the government had applied the National Security Provisions."

"National Security Provisions?" I echoed, and Jemenga grumbled his low laugh.

"I forget your provincial environment." He gestured grandly with his long arms. "But surely even this rustic hamlet is aware of the rudiments of the N.S.P.?"

"Afraid not. You speak, you realize, to one who is both a country bumpkin and an ivory-tower intellectual." That primitive quip earned a crockery-rattling laugh. The doctor was in a good mood, almost certainly freshly viewing the mental image of himself delivering his acceptance speech at the Kalinidor banquet. "Excuse me," I added.

I thumped to my feet and around to the doorway, from which, with a little stretching, I could wriggle my fingers to the corner of my desk. I snaked my review copy across the table to Jemenga.

"What's this?" he wondered, scanning the text in his rapid, almost mechanical reading style. Then, "You subversive know-it-all!" he laughed, his voice rumbling lower and resonating in the small tiled kitchen. "How did you get away with this?"

I shrugged, feigning a doltish expression. "Us country bumpkins is just lucky." Then I hunkered down again over my cup. "Sure you won't have any? I have honey to spare."

He waved a negative, and proceeded to read through my paper … officially, Tkonle's student's paper.

As he read, I felt a new anxiety rumbling through me. What was all this about National Security? How would that affect me? What would they want to do to Haillyen? And could my aunts tolerate me if it became known that a Varayla was afraid of the Government?

# 9

*"Outrageous. There I was, about to be beaten to publication.
And by whom? My water-carrier."*

– Eskanyan Jemenga
Physician-Scholar

W HILE MY MIND RAN THROUGH all the potential consequences of running afoul of this National Security business, Jemenga calmly read through my paper. Reassuringly, he telegraphed only interest, not alarm or disdain.

"Jemenga," I said, finally. "Tell me now. What does it mean, this declassification?"

He waved a marginally rude reply with his left hand. I waited, impatient, and consoled myself with extra honey. Finally, he set the paper aside.

"Not bad," he said. "But mine will be better." He leaned back on his haunches and gave me what I took to be a severe looking-over. "What you ask…well, better I should be asking you how this managed to get by the R.P."

"Who?"

"The Reportage Police." He tapped his fingers on my bold treatise (which also satisfied a course requirement under my latest mentoring contract with Tkonle). "It is supposed that they read everything submitted for publication. I confess I never considered the consequences of that supposition. If they truly read everything, there would be more R.P.'s than anything else. I hereby revise my suppositions to presume that review is selective and targets topics likely to tie into current security concerns. Nonverbal communication has historically been the province of the addled and the eccentric."

"Yes, yes, I know all the jibes by heart already. Try this one. 'What's the difference between a madman and a philosopher?'"

"Do tell, my dear demented one."

I had to laugh myself at that, but managed to deliver the standard one-liner. "The madman says 'Hah! What's the difference?' and the philosopher says, 'Huh? What do you mean by *difference*?'"

Jemenga gestured a smile, but he didn't laugh. "Seriously, you are fortunate that this will be released after the declassification is finalized. Once published, if it earns you and your mentor the attention it merits, it will be subject to review."

"For what?" I stood and stretched. "Listen, Jemenga, you are making me both confused and worried. I am going for a walk. Care to accompany me?"

There was more to my feelings at the moment, and not all was as open to discussion as competing academic papers. Jemenga graciously followed my lead. I was not even surprised at that until thinking over our discussion later on.

"I'm worried about Haillyen," I said as soon as we were safely out of listening distance. "She's taken to some odd behaviors of late." True to form, Jemenga merely lowered his eyes to the path and allowed me to get on with it. "She's obsessed with a mirror, one I gave her some time ago, when I first became caught up in some bad reasoning about sentience and nonsentience. Lately, she spends every free moment staring into it. I've happened on her making odd faces into it, but as soon as she's aware I'm there, she stops and pretends simply to be looking at her reflection."

I sighed, wrapped my arms around my waist, and stopped. We were at the edge of the stream by then. A couple of long strides and a hop and I was over. Jemenga stared at me, then.

"You expect me to prance over a brook like a child of ten?" he said.

I waved a long shrug. "This is the path. After all that tramping in the wilderness, are you afraid of a little garden stream, now?"

He huffed and puffed, but he followed. "There is a noticeable age difference, here."

I laughed. "What do you mean, 'difference'?"

He took it well enough. In silence, we hiked on to the top of the little knoll beyond the stream. Technically, we were trespassing on the farm next door, but I was privy to knowledge that the Family had a controlling interest in the company who owned the firm that held the land leases. Not to mention that Farmer Tokal was an old friend from childhood. We had committed many sins of property together in the long fruitful summers.

The view from the knoll was one of my favorites. Behind, of course, stood my own little paradise, the house nestling close under a wide-spreading entelebar tree. But outward, to the west, lay a pastoral panorama of the South Tule Directorate. I knew all the farms and most of the farmers. The patchwork colors of the local variety of crops at various stages of growth gave the valley a restful blend of texture and hue. The mountains beyond framed the tame and comfortable farmland with seemingly untamed wilderness.

Every time I strolled up to take in that dose of heart's-ease, I swore to become a painter so that I could capture its appeal. At sunset, I would swear it twice over.

I said as much to Jemenga, who said, "Well, my boy, we're fortunate it's early yet for the artistic demands of sunset."

The doctor is no connoisseur of inspiring scenery. He gave the view a few seconds of polite gazing and commented only, "Pretty, yes." Then he looked back, down the steep slope towards my challenging little stream. "However, I can see that this might help you create the proper frame of mind for completing our paper."

"Yes, yes, I suppose it might," I said with a frustrated sigh. As a nascent communication expert, I should have been able to communicate a simple concern. "I come for the pleasure in the view. I need it quite often, Jemenga." My fingers started twitching again, nervous wriggles. I looped my arms together, trying to calm the muscles, but still felt as if I had a handful of panicked worms tangled below my carpus node. "How do I explain? I feel so … so …" and I concluded with an eloquent wriggly shrug of confusion.

"Ah! That!" So, my self-revelation was to be greeted with one of Jemenga's patented belly laughs. Oh, well.

But he didn't laugh. Instead, he prodded *my* belly. He stuck his medically-certified manipulatives in my eyes and ear fronds. He made me open my mouth, and studied the interior as if he'd a mind to extract some of that upper-class chewing-surface. He reviewed my eating habits, not to mention recycling habits.

Then Jemenga laced his professorial fingers together and said with some gravity, "I know what ails you, my boy. Seen it a hundred times. Are you listening?"

I nodded, all my attention focused on him. Even the view, which had begun to warm into a pink glow, I demoted to second place.

"First ..." he ticked off diagnoses on his left hand, "first, you have About-To-Publish Anxiety Syndrome. This is self-resolving. As soon as I ... or, I suppose, your Mentor ... get you working on new material, you will revert to your normal anxiety state.

"Second ... you have a communication problem with your housemate." At my offended stare, he waved his right hand dismissively. "You are getting ahead of me! To solve this communication problem, a common occurrence among students sharing living quarters, it is necessary to apply and extend the content of your soon-to-be-published paper. I have every confidence that Haillyen has an explanation for her behavior, and that it is more than reasonable.

"Third ... I observe here an acute—need I say debilitating—case of Bachelor Distress."

"What? You want me to get *married?* Have you been talking to Aunt Ansele?"

"Oh, my, no! What woman would want you in such a state? Imagine the note on the social registry bulletin board: *Obsessively anxious man with weird housemate seeks permanent relief from year-long spate of unnatural celibacy.* No, no, no. I merely point to the remarkable shift in activity in that area of your life."

Jemenga has a positive talent for arousing embarrassment in others. Normally, this is exercised in a scientific way, asking the one question that tears away the foundation of a rival's set of theories. But now I was grateful for the growing color of the sky and the fast-approaching mountain shadow. I'm sure I was as pale as a ghost. I know I was less than civil.

"I think," I said stiffly. "I think it's time to go back to the house." I executed a smooth, haughty turn-on-haunches, but found Jemenga blocking the trail.

"Don't go thundering off," he said.

Even in the swiftly fading light, I could tell his color was off as well. What had Jemenga to worry about?

"Listen first," he went on. "Then run if you need to. Do you think you are the only person who has ever had such difficulties?" And he thumped me on the chest, not terribly hard, but enough that I halted, glaring at him, feeling the cold shades of anger flood my face.

"Start with Item Three," he said. "Think it through for yourself. Where are all the friends your aunts complained of so? Have you had even one visitor here who came for the pleasure of your company only, not to deliver goods or care for Haillyen?"

"Huh," I grunted. "Do you think I would have any of those fellows around? They are nothing but bubble-heads!"

A few of the old comrades had stopped by, early on. None could cope with the presence of the alien creature. One managed to depart unscathed; two others made the mistake of offending with their sophomoric little jokes and carried home a few bruises. My darling Turame? I still recall how the bruises she left on my heart ached at Jemenga's query.

I turned again, back to that calming outlook. The afternoon clouds had become shining golden streamers. Would any of those old school chums have even appreciated this? Would they have felt that thrill in their guts watching the gold flow to scarlet before their eyes?

"You're right, of course," I said, finally, low and respectful. "But the old friends are no good anymore, and how am I to make new friends? Let alone a … a …." I sighed.

"The prescription is simple. You must get out yourself, see people, interact with them. Some will turn out to be friends. You have the knack, my boy, you are just too isolated here to exercise it."

"But I can't leave Haillyen!" I protested. I twisted to peer back to the house, just in time to see the light come on over the back garden.

"She can take care of herself. If you fear for her safety, rich boy, hire her a bodyguard! But get yourself out! Make Tkonle take you to a conference. Trot down to the town library and ask for help researching the National Security regulations. Play ball—I see people out on the fields every time I come over. They have a good facility, because of the planned mini-town just north of your beautiful view. Take advantage!

"Meanwhile, remember the cure for Item Two. You must practice what you preach in your anxiety-producing paper. Talk to your housemate. You've successfully managed to communicate everything from basic greetings to dinner menus. You should certainly be able to find out what this odd behavior means!

"From there it is an easy leap back to Item One. In solidarity with every other first-year Student Scholar, you are obsessed with the possible failure of what is only the first entry in what will be a splendid list of hundreds of publications. For your own benefit, I propose that you buckle down and finish our paper for me, as swiftly as you may. Then you will have two papers behind you."

I absorbed all this advice quietly, my eyes on the sunset, which had slipped away from the low clouds to reveal a much higher layer of fractured cirrus. A good sunset, I decided, a memorable one.

"It's a pity to waste such a perfectly progressing sunset on a self-serving codger like you," I said, barely even conscious of my fingers shaping the smile. "Let's go in before the trail is too dark for your aging eyes."

He looked closely at me, trying, I knew, to pick out the color changes in that poor light. I took the opportunity to thump him back.

"There!" I said. "In the good old days, I'd have kicked you on your heels for that."

He said only, "Oof!" Then, a little too late to be realistic, he produced a dramatic moan.

"Let's go," I laughed.

At the creek, he showed off a lovely leaping style.

"Hold on there," I said. "What happened to your aging musculature?"

"Hah!" he said. "Got you there! You've boasted convincingly of your skill on the ballfield. My own sport was field events. I was a premium hurdler in my day. Medaled in cross-country, as well."

"You did not!"

"I did! I swear it!"

"Never!"

The cool shades of evening fell across the sky as we strolled together up the slope to the house.

# 10

*"Naturally, he turned to me for help. I could never say no to that boy. My sister finds fault in my vulnerability, and her reasons are well-founded. But especially as a youngster, he so reminded me of our dear departed brother."*

– Varayla Adeleke
CEO, Varayla Industries

HAILLYEN WAS WAITING FOR US, standing in the open doorway. Once again, I was reminded of the days of my childhood, when it would be Cook there at the door, feigning impatience while enjoying a glass of something sweet and fermented. She'd always deliver a stern lecture, countered by the conspiratorial grin she'd deliver with her free hand, always ending with, "One of these days, boy, I'll not turn on the garden light, and there you'll be, lost in the dark."

A light flickered in the back of my mind. Now, then, who had been minding that garden light all those other evenings these past several months, even when I'd lingered until the sunset was cool?

As always, Jemenga greeted Haillyen as not only a person, but an equal. He wrapped his hands around hers, fairly dragged her to the parlor, and consumed a half-hour speaking energetically to the both of us on the urgency of the work he required of me.

To be sure, I needed no persuading, but it was a pure pleasure to lean back and watch Haillyen absorb this entertainment. She watched him intently, apparently listening closely. She even seemed to echo his gestures, as people do, though her bony arms and fingers made for jerky movements.

When he pressed my paper into her hands, and launched into a series of anecdotes of first-year Scholars whose early efforts had failed, but who ultimately became famous, she bent her head over "Non-Universality of Color-Based Communication" and moved her finger across the lines. With another little internal flicker of intelligence, I wondered if it would be easier for her injured brain to learn reading than it was to recapture speech. Were the two functions separate enough?

So, my head was full of competing notions as Jemenga made excuses about staying for supper. He seemed tempted; there was a paper he pulled out of his case twice and stuffed back in, reconsidering. His look became odd, distracted. He claimed to have some issues urgently requiring his attention at home, and he departed while I was still itemizing candidate menus.

Later, while dinner bubbled in the oven, I paged through the contents of the little hand-comp Jemenga had left behind. It was indeed the actual notepad we'd had on the expedition. I recognized the scratched screen and dented case. Jemenga's own files were, I knew, safely stored and catalogued in top-of-the-line equipment.

There would be time enough tomorrow to tackle the anatomical analyses he'd dictated at the time. Where were my own philological entries? Sure enough, I had saved the screen images from that day Haillyen and I had experimented with writing. I trotted through the parlor to her room.

"Haillyen," I called as I went. "Come look at this. Do you remember this?"

But when I reached her doorway, there she was, leaning up to the mirror, her face twisted in some alien expression, her arms moving jerkily as if she were rehearsing some avant-garde dance form.

The long-quiescent image of the twisting tendrils flashed across the front of my brain. I fought it down, forcing myself to think of Jemenga's simple and sage advice. *We really should talk about this*, I thought. *But how?*

"Haillyen," I said, stepping into the room and trying to shape an easy smile. "What is all this about? Is there a problem I can help you with?"

But at my first syllable, she froze. Then her arms shifted to more normal positioning. She patted at her head-fur, as if arranging it. And she made that toothy mouth-smile of hers. I hesitated, and almost pursued the issue. But, I don't know why, that smile stopped me. It seemed every bit as false a smile as the one frozen on my fingertips.

*If it were madness, or even possession by alien brain whatsits,* I told myself, *it wouldn't embarrass her to have me see this. Whatever it is, it's something private.* So instead I held up the hand-comp to show her the screen with her handwriting on it. "Remember this?"

Her expression changed, and the smile became real. With a little shiver of delight, I was startled to realize why—with her awkward right hand, despite its inadequate fingers, she was tracing a very readable approximation of a proper smile. Then she reached out for the old notepad, found the stylus, and traced over the letters she had drawn that day.

"Wonderful!" I said, though the tracing was shakier than the original. I pulled up a blank screen. "Want to do some more?" I challenged.

Dinner that night was slightly stale bread and reheated soup. My casserole—a dish of my own invention that usually earned full attention—had burned beyond recognition by the time we left off. We didn't even take ourselves to the relative comfort of the parlor, but spent the evening parked on her sleeping mat, itemizing nouns. It is purely surprising how many words there are in a simple country house.

The next morning, first thing, I wrote to Jemenga. Applying all my recently-acquired skill in Scholarese, I formally accepted his proposal to complete the first paper in our joint effort of describing the one and only First Contact achieved by the Transfer Project. I inserted the necessary boilerplate language needed to reserve certain rights for research currently under my own purview. Then it was signed, sealed, and ready to go off to the post on the grocer's cart that afternoon.

But of course, until Jemenga executed his half of the paperwork, there was no contract in place. I was not obligated to page over to those creepy surgical commentaries of his. And I had something else to occupy my interest. By the time Haillyen emerged looking for breakfast (I no longer even wondered if all her kind required so much sleep), I was well into a thesis proposal to Tkonle, playing up the potential for multiple publications in the course of a work involving development of interspecies communication in written form.

Already, I was sagacious enough about the scholar's world to know that if this project were to be my thesis, it would be *my* name first on all those publications. Yes, Jemenga was right. It was turning to future work that had cured me of fussing over the completed effort.

While Haillyen ate, I turned on the over-priced, little-used telephone and called Aunt Adeleke.

"Auntie," I said, in my most flattering tones, positioning myself for the best camera angle, so she could observe my happy, confident colors and my well-trained, dance-quality gestures. "I was wondering if there might possibly be sitting around the office any disused flat-panel engineer's comps? An outdated model would be wonderful for me . . . I just need something suited to drawing, but all I have is Jemenga's old hand-comp."

She was cool-toned, skeptical, but I could detect her curiosity behind it all. "What are you up to now, boy? You can't make a living on art, any more than you could on poetry!"

I considered being teasingly vague. Adeleke had often indulged my little whims in the past, always interested in just how much of a disaster I could produce. Instead, I went for directness.

"Not art, Auntie. I'm working on a project that requires some sketches. Actually, it's two projects, one with Jemenga. You remember him, don't you? Senior Dean of Scholars in Residence at Utumwe? Medical Practitioner of the Year? And the other will be my thesis. You know, a Scholar-in-Practice work."

She affected a shocked expression. Her self-control is legendary, but I could still detect a little warmth about her eyes. And her gestures had that faintly motherly quality that let me know I was making progress. "This is disturbing," she temporized. "You have never before proposed any action that might complete your schooling. Are you ill?"

"Not at all ma'am. I am merely reverting to my normal behavior. Haven't I wheedled goodies from you all my short life?"

"So you have. So you have."

She stared at me out of the screen. I knew she was looking for the signs of incipient failure. I knew she could recount the entire litany of my false starts and backslides. And she always saw through my jokes.

"All right," she decided. "There is always junk lying around. I will have my secretary look for something you can use."

"Thank you!"

Her look was still sharp, calculating. "It goes in the accounts," she said firmly. "It is a recordable donation to your mentor's scholar-support account."

I nearly laughed.

"Yes, of course." And I made myself a mental note: *Think of that angle first, next time.* Suddenly, Aunt Adeleke's expression changed. An unfamiliar shade tinged the edges of her face ... was that confusion or consternation? My ear fronds quivered at a soft sound behind me, and I turned.

Haillyen stood there, looking back at Auntie. Surely they'd seen each other before? Then I noticed Haillyen's toothy grin and paired it with her right hand, which, as I watched, sketched her much-improved smile of greeting.

"I see," said Adeleke. And with her well-tooled manners, her legendary self-control, she sent back her own polite smile. Then she quickly signed off. Business called.

Business indeed. Who was busier? Auntie with her mega-buck, mega-staff, mega-widget company, or the pair of us with our scavenged flatscreen?

As promised, she sent a well-used device, but it was still top-of-the-line, and it arrived via the grocer's cart by the end of the week. At that point, Haillyen and I had already applied the more primitive hand-comp to make an inventory of nouns for most of the items in the house. I barely even quailed at asking the grocery boy to show me how to connect the old and new devices. I swear he laughed all the way up the road, but I didn't care one whit.

Jemenga's reply to my contract proposal came, too, in the same cart load. But somehow, I could not find enough time to jump into his piece of work. There were those cold shivers and writhing, dark dreams that woke me up in the night. There was that queasy sensation when Haillyen bent over to pick up a dropped stylus and I caught a glimpse of the pink, wrinkled scar tissue usually concealed by her head fur. Picking up Jemenga's contract gave me those same feelings, so somehow it gathered dust on the side table.

Meanwhile, Haillyen was anxious to start on verbs. I, however, was determined to turn our beginning inventory into a dictionary. So, she would poke me in the shoulder and mime some action. I would point at the flatscreen and demonstrate adding another inane sketch to illustrate an object. Then she would poke me again, until I provided the word that went with the movement she wanted to define.

The third time through this cycle, I could feel myself darkening up and getting stiff with the effort to keep at my project. "Listen," I declared. "We have to be organized about this. We have to be methodical. We have to take notes! You can't possibly just remember all this! You're going to need a dictionary!"

It was useless to object. It only made her more excited. She tapped the screen urgently, gestured at my face, mimed a ferocious beast with snarling teeth and outstretched claws.

"What?" I protested. "What do you want *now?*"

She made herself calmer, and then she carefully ran one outstretched finger along the color streaks on my face, tracing the slowly fading hues of my outburst.

"Oh," and she watched with that intent look as I faded into embarrassed understanding. "It's adjectives you want now. All right." And I carefully printed out *angry*. Then I sketched in a very crude face, thanked Aunty for the top-line full-color flatscreen, and tinted in my best approximation of my own deep-shaded purple anger.

Suddenly, I realized a link there. I sketched in, as best I could, an array of emotive colorations. At least, I covered the basics: fear, happiness, humor, sadness. And, in turn, she displayed for me her own facial expressions. At last I was able to directly confirm—or, more often, *disprove*—the mere guesses I'd put into my faulty first paper. Emotive expression for her included facial movements, body language, and even … I called up my notes from our first few days together … vocal pitch.

For a solid week, we worked like a pair of kazeran in a hauling race. Together, we focused entirely on the dictionary. I relented in my demands to follow my style of logic; she had her own method, it was clear. What Haillyen demanded were sufficient components to assemble basic sentences as soon as possible. Clearly a long list of nouns was not suitable for her plans.

What that meant was that, in no time at all, she was talking. Well, communicating in writing. And I don't mean anything indirect or subtle. It was. "Ansegwe, get dinner now." And, "Fried fish taste bad." And, "More work, now."

At the end of the fifth day, I came back to the parlor from assembling a pot of stew, and found her clutching the flatscreen close to her chest. Her eyes were overflowing; her breathing was ragged.

"Oh, no!" I cried. "When did this come on? Is the damned humidifier broken *again*?"

I was about to stamp out, to rummage for my tools once more, but just then she looked up at me. And she smiled, a real smile, smooth and graceful with practice. She fumbled for the stylus and wrote swiftly, if raggedly.

*Ansegwe angry no. You unhappy no. Haillyen do ...* and she hesitated and wrote ... *water eyes. I happy. Water eyes sad or happy. Now is happy happy happy. Machine bad not.*

I know I turned green. I know it because she pointed at me, made her burbly noise, and then wrote. *Good. Ansegwe happy. I stop water eyes. Laugh now.*

# 11

*"Staffing Requirement #7: one individual, of short stature and low mass, with Translation Shift experience, skilled in Tkonlevian non-verbal communication techniques."*

— RFP TFP-9071-4fg

H AILLYEN LOOKED UP AT ME with those tiny little eyes of hers glistening with … with … happiness?

*Laugh now*, she'd said. I couldn't help it. I did laugh. I couldn't remember ever laughing so hard. I think the crockery in the kitchen rattled. All that money and work on the air conditioning system, while I was supposedly doing landmark research in nonverbal communication, and what she was doing all those sad, frustrating times, was weeping. I tried to remember if her eyes really did water when she seemed happy, too. How could such a dramatic, messy form of expression mean two opposite things?

Inspired, I snatched the flatscreen, and I saved that display. *That's a breakthrough*, I told myself, but I knew it was just my sentimental side taking charge. *I don't ever want to forget this.*

Then it was my turn, and it was about time for this conversation. Limited vocabulary be damned. *Haillyen do arm moves, look in mirror, do face happy? Sad? Angry? Tell Ansegwe.*

She stilled her own laughter and studied my message. She even was careful, tapped to the dictionary to check on 'mirror'. But an answer was not forthcoming. Somehow, I could tell by the way she failed to start scribbling immediately. I could feel myself fading, and she glanced up at me, and I knew then that she could tell my moods.

Finally, she did write a short response: *Not now.*

I couldn't think of a good answer for that. I wanted to be angry. I certainly was disappointed. And there she was staring at me, watching me, absorbing information. She tugged the screen back and scrawled, *Work now. Talk dinner.*

At first, it was difficult to get back to work. My concentration was poor. I had to keep getting up. At one point, I jerked to my feet, trotted back to my room, and spent a restless half-hour sprawled on my sleeping mat, telling myself to nap while my mind worried at half-baked notions for framing an explanation of syntax.

Finally, it dawned on me that successful use of syntax required more than a mass of words sorted into a dictionary. She needed more context, intonation, and conceptual structure in order to communicate even something as simple as "Let's talk after dinner." Or "Tell me what you've got planned for dinner." Or "I'm working on that now." Or even "I'm hungry."

So, still feeling awkward and rejected and cranky, I pushed up from my mat and trudged back to the parlor. She was hard at work (or was it work, really?) drawing cartoons on the screen. I leaned over her shoulder (and how strange to be so accustomed to doing that).

Yes, she had moved on to adjectives and conceptual verbs. There were a half-dozen faces (my kind, not hers) sketched on the screen. One she had surrounded with snaky little symbols. One had a picture floating in a bubble over it. Another had a little box next to it with a series of numbers: 1, 2, 3. The fourth also had a list of numbers, but each number had a meaningless scribble after it—like words written too small to resolve.

I was drawn in. "That one's thinking about doing some things in order, isn't he?" I guessed. "Let's call that plan." And I looped one hand around, grasped her hand in mine and wrote out the word.

The other three words, we were not so sure on, but I felt more confident overall. With some usage, we'd find out our errors. Some guesses would lead to more errors than others. We'd just have to try to build from simple ideas in order to be able to discuss more complicated ones.

Dinner was quiet, but not gloomy. I felt too pleased with the afternoon's work to broach my question again.

But avoiding the issue made me anxious, of course. That meant that after dinner I went out for one of my walks. It was a long walk, looping around the whole property and along my favorite cut-throughs on the neighbors' leases. By the time the midsummer sun was starting to dip towards the horizon, I had climbed to my favorite spot, ready for the sky to perform my favorite show.

I made it in time for the first tinge of sunset—and my luck held. It was a particularly good sequence, from a delicate spread of hue all around the circle of the sky, caught in the low, thin clouds that had cooled the day so inefficiently, to a glorious blaze around a thunderhead constructing itself just south of the sun. I phrased a few lines of poetry in my head and wondered if I could remember them long enough to write them down.

Then a flicker of brightness across the face of the thunderhead reminded me to get moving. The top of a hill would not be the best location to watch a lightning storm. So off I went down the slope, muttering my few lines to myself by way of memorization.

Just as I was about to bound over the stream, I spotted her. Haillyen was sitting at the edge of the stream. She dabbled her odd floppy feet in the water, those fingerlike stubs wiggling in the coolness. I toned down my dramatic leap to a more decorous hop and crouched down beside her. "Hello," I said.

It was nearly dark, but with the garden light filtering down from the house, I could see her smile. She had the flatscreen, and was busily writing on it. I waited. For once, I felt a touch of patience. Maybe it was the sunset poem swirling gently around my mind.

Finally, she simply handed me the big comp. And waited. I found it difficult to see in the bad light, and bumped up the illumination. There was a lot on that one screen, written small in her wavery hand.

*You want Haillyen talk arms in mirror face in mirror. Want talk. Need talk you person talk. You talk arms mouth skin. My person talk mouth. Arms not good, arms got sticks inside, bad shape. Skin not good, color bad. Work work work for talk. Color bad, no good.*

*Arms do little good. Smile good now. Mouth not work. Not make my person words. Not make you person words. I write words now. Words not wait. Haillyen need go. Need get friend. Bad person hurt friend, hurt Haillyen. Haillyen talk now. I go get friend.*

The need to jump up and take another walk was nearly overwhelming. My self-control was rewarded with a wave of nausea. I felt as if the earth under my curled-up legs had decided to go for a walk without me.

I stared at the glowing screen. It seemed to be floating in front of me, as the twilight faded to early evening. I noticed an erratic tapping sound, but then realized it was my own hand, tapping the stylus on that word: *go.*

Questions clustered in my mind, crowding around the core interrogatives *where? how? when?* The swirling sensation of disorientation persisted, making me glad I was already sitting down. I coiled my arm around the flatscreen and stared at it as if more information was going to appear any second.

All these weeks, probably since the day Tumbal had pronounced her fit enough and wheeled away in his tiny little runabout, she had been struggling to obtain enough vocabulary to ask for a ride home. In the meantime, I had been settling into a comfortable, academic domesticity. She was inextricably linked with all my half-baked plans.

That old heart's-pain billowed up inside. She would go. Where would that leave me?

More alone than ever. More alone than the little boy sitting by this stream for the very first time, all those many years ago, weeping for the loss of the Bad Parents. More alone than the happy-go-lucky perpetual student toying with love and money. More alone than the unwanted explorer on the most unsuccessful Transfer Mission ever.

My ears hurt. Suddenly, I realized I'd scrunched them in so hard I couldn't hear a thing. I relaxed them out a bit, soaked in the soft gurgle of the stream flowing by. I could hear her too, again, and Haillyen's breathing had that rough, wet quality I'd just learned meant either happiness or sadness. Which was it?

Under cover of unwrapping my nearly-numb arm from the flatscreen, I peeked over at Haillyen. The glow from the screen cast a bright enough light to see. Sure enough, there were those streaks of moisture running down from her eyes, gathering at the edge where that long jawbone cut the lines of her face, and dripping off onto her clothing. Something in the set of her mouth told me this was not happy weeping. Finally, I summoned up some speech of my own.

"Go?" I managed to choke out. "So. You need to leave. We need to rescue your friend. How can I help?" And my hand, as if operated by a magic demon out of myth, copied my words onto the screen.

•  •  •

It wasn't just my help she needed. The Family might have had a small interest in the Transfer Project, but that was no Syndicate enterprise. It was a multi-national cooperative venture, the ultimate in multi-layered regulatory environments. As a spare unit, tossed onto the expedition at the last minute, I had had no opportunities to observe these machinations the first time around.

Ah, but now I was a skilled veteran of the Medical System—a far more ancient and arcane society. I knew the rules. Have your forms in order, by all means. But neglect not the necessity of persuasion from upper levels. Apply force in phased layers.

Tkonle, successful purveyor of student enterprise, credentialed and internationally renowned in his field, launched the opening salvo with, not a proposal, but (the canny beast!) a Request for Proposals, suitable for a Groundbreaking Work in the Field.

Jemenga, master at all times of his immediate environs and all environs potentially attachable to his territory, floated a grant application at the Emirate of Quazwallade, a non-signer of the Consolidation, but a noisy and influential nation with a monopoly on certain highly-valued resources. The Emir had a fancy to be a part of the Consolidation's grand futuristic ventures; an investment in TransComm suited the budget he'd allotted.

By happy coincidence, Jemenga's colleague on the Kalinidor-nominated "Expeditionary Report, Medical and Contact Crews, Project VA-01-34 (Declassified 8.7.5497)" was able to secure an extraordinarily unusual individual to fill out the Staffing section of his Proposal Response.

And as usual, but this time last of all, I applied to my darling aunties for a few gentle nudges to the appropriate officials. Ansele did not have to tell me her feelings; she positively radiated in the cyan. All those years, when I had been so forthrightly, honestly idle, it had been my lack of the family deviousness that had troubled her mind. At last I was proven a true scion of the Varayla family tree.

Not that any of this happened quickly. Time gets away from us, in real life. There are meals to be cooked, walks to realign the nerves, long ligament-straining journeys to Town to pitch the project, and, most important of all, cubic acres of paperwork to be completed. It was a year before we were ready.

# 12

*"I took him for one more regretful college dropout. The poor fellow was utterly hopeless at finding his way around the reference catalog. Or so Ans'we led me to believe."*

- Ensense Kantalare
Curator, Korlo Interactive Museum

DID I SAY IT TOOK A YEAR? Make that another year, rather. From the beginning, from the first sound of shouts on the hillside, to the day we set foot once again on that strangely familiar world with its strangely unfamiliar creatures in it, fully two years passed. But just as the first year is indelible and clear to me, the second is a dazed blur. Perhaps I am constitutionally unable to store memories without sufficient rest, peace, and quiet.

But a few clear sequences rise up out of the murk.

·    ·    ·

There was that evening—midsummer I think it was—when I was staying up late working out schedules. I had parked myself out on the rear terrace, to catch the last traces of the summer sunset. Haillyen flicked on the lights. I complained. The twilight returned and the door clanged as she came out to join me.

"What is all this about?" she asked, once she managed to drag my eyes from the sky and down to her screen.

I tapped up the scheduling charts. The logistics and maneuverings were complex. "Look," I said, pointing her along one trace in the tree. "That's us, what we need to be doing to prepare.

"For instance, here, that's where we get our joint paper done, so Tkonle can apply his endorsement to it, so we can get a pass-through from the Approvals Committee at the regular monthly meeting . . . here.

"That approval's flagged in blue, since it's critical. Without that, we'll either be held up until the next meeting or we'll have to appear in person, which will create too many additional questions along the lines of 'What? *That's* your Expert?' See?"

By way of answer, Haillyen simply tapped up my ancient graphic describing "boredom." Then, a little more charitably, she added "Not my idea of a good time, making these pictures. But yes, right, I see the paper has to get done."

"Good, good. And it has to be both of us together, do you see? For the Approval Committee. Both of us need the approval, so we can both go, otherwise the Committee could appoint some other Communication Expert." And I looked up at her and laughed. "Wouldn't want some popular lardhead like Tselegard tramping off into the woods with you instead. His public might miss him."

She treated me to another of her mysterious, silent looks. She didn't share a laugh, not even her high-pitched squeaky one. Instead, she reached out to my comp, tapped in a file-save command and turned the machine off. I hardly had a chance to twitch an objection before she scribbled, "Come inside. Cold out here."

Mystified, I followed her. Was she some kind of scheduling expert at home? Had I made a fatal error of some kind?

Haillyen led me to the kitchen and balanced on her chair, the flatscreen on the table in front of her. She was clearly agitated. She kept beginning to write and tapping erase, putting down the flatscreen and picking it up again.

I reached out and rested one arm across her shoulders. "What is wrong?" I asked, trying to conceal my own rising concern. She glanced up at me, sighed, and bent over her comp once again.

"Tell me," she wrote. "Do you plan to go with me, to find Az-dyel, to go to my home?"

I was taken aback. What had she imagined I planned? "Of course!" I said. "What else?" I forced a laugh. "You weren't planning on going alone, were you?"

She bent her head down on that long flexible neck. Her fur dangled over her face. She wrote furiously.

"Yes. I go alone. This is not for you. I do not come back. There are no people like you out there. How do you think it will be, all alone?"

"That's ridiculous. I get you home. I come back. End of story. It's too dangerous for you alone."

She shook her head, side to side, so the long fur flopped over her eyes. "More danger with you. What would the Stick Men do, with you there? What will they see? Do you think they will want to *talk* to you?"

"But … but … what they did to you … before. Have you lost your memory as well as your common sense?"

She had a ready answer. "That was those certain people only. Those people, they knew Az-dyel. Or Az-dyel knew them. And I was strange to them, so … so … colorless."

"This is stupid. You're heading straight for *those* people. Straight back to that trouble. And you think you don't need help?"

As usual, I was having trouble sorting out my feelings. But her readings of my emotions were accurate, and her stylus flew over the screen.

"Stop being jealous. I will need help. But you will not help me. You will make them frightened. You will get angry and cause trouble. I know other people there, too, people who will help me. And these people, I know they can help me get home. Just help me get out there, where I can find Az-dyel and these people. Hyooman people like me. Please." And she looked up at me directly, finally. "You will still help me go, won't you?"

What could I say? I had no choice. "Yes."

•      •      •

Then there was that morning in late fall, when Jemenga arrived with one arm coiled securely around his latest stack of reports and the other dangling an empty packbag. He gave me no opportunity to frame a joke or even a question; Haillyen took the bag before Jemenga had his front feet on the step.

"What do you need that for?" I asked.

"I'm going up to town with Jemenga," she scrawled on the screen. Her writing had become sloppier as lately she had become more involved with what she had to say than how it got said. "It will take a few days," she went on. "You keep on working."

When they disappeared at the end of the lane, and I turned back to the house, its quietude and solitude suddenly seemed more like emptiness. Cooking did not appeal, with no one to share the food. The work wouldn't settle. The video was mindless and aimless and pointless. All of my books were already read and remembered.

So, I went down to the little town, just up the road from the village. I found my way to the small, but modern, library. The golden-skinned goddess in charge of the reference department shunned me, at first, as an interloper, an irregular. But by closing time, a spark of the old Ansegwe had ignited enough interest for an exchange of names.

I visited Kantalare's domain again the very next day.

On the third day, the beautiful librarian was looking out for me. Kantalare had already pulled the documents that would naturally follow from the items I'd requested the previous day. Lunch was in order. And there was no question of charming her with my exploits. I was too fascinated by the endless string of yarns K'alare had to tell of crackpots and wild-armed loonies invading the staid little country library with requests for the details of non-existent government plots and maps describing the locations of hidden treasure. We never got around to Ansegwe's story that day.

But we got around each other, soon enough.

There came a time when I barely noticed just how much time Haillyen was spending in town. I did recognize it enough to make a few remarks about her "budding" relationship with Jemenga. But such attempts at humor only made Haillyen turn that confusing shade of pink and vanish into her room.

I actually began to wonder—just to myself, not daring enough to share the notion with K'alare—if the joke was not a joke. Both Jemenga and Haillyen seemed to grow bubblier every time I saw them.

There were those evenings, then, when we would have Jemenga and my sweet K'alare to dinner. Without exception, at some point in the meal, Haillyen and Jemenga would glance at each other, begin a gesture, and perhaps even (in the good doctor's case) begin to speak. Then they would abruptly break off that exchange, Jemenga huffing down a laugh and Haillyen barely covering her uniquely high-pitched *keegle* of a laugh.

One evening, I was in a just-shy-of-sober state and interrupted her with a sloshy "Stop that keegling, you." Of course, I expected that Jemenga would whisper something about my chemical state, and they would really laugh at me. All of them.

But I was wrong.

"No, I won't." Haillyen said, aloud, with the proper matching negative gesture. The words were thick, a little too precisely enunciated, reminding me of a tourist's accent, or evoking a person fighting through a respiratory infection. To belabor the point: this was not the foreign language I'd heard when we first met. It was her rendition of mine.

All of them observed my reactions with undisguised amusement and pleasure. K'alare herself stifled a laugh and glowed with her most pleasing colors. I forced myself to glare at her.

"You were in on this? How?" At least she had the good grace to curl her left arm apologetically around her waist.

"Only for a short while. You remember, just a week or so ago, when you were late returning from that conference, and were so worried about a delivery of books or papers coming in the next day." She lifted those deep amber eyes to mine, coaxing me to recall that day.

The collusion fell into place. The call she'd taken from Jemenga, who'd been unaware I had been delayed. As usual, they'd framed the view so I'd be able to see Haillyen looking over his shoulder, ready to gesture her familiar hello to me. Though perhaps K'alare hadn't the experience to recognize Haillyen's expression, I could readily envision those little eyes spreading wide while Jemenga's colors flickered through surprise to amusement. But the punchline I couldn't have predicted: Haillyen blurting out a clear, if ungrammatical, "What she doing there?" complete with her barely-polite version of the interrogative gesture.

Congratulations were in order, and I delivered as best I could. But my colors were a poor match to my confused feelings, I knew.

Puzzlement was only the surface effect—naturally, I had a deep need to know how they'd accomplished this feat. But also, there was the dismay at realizing that a flaw had opened in my own secret scheme. I had been sure that Haillyen would have to take me along, in the end. How could she have insisted on traveling alone, when she couldn't even speak without a fragile mechanical aid? My thoughts tunneled deep, and I struggled to channel every shred of positive thinking to the surface. Now, I would have to pin my hopes to accompany her on trickery and deception, notably not my foremost skills.

At least I had not been the one responsible for the utter failure of our Medical Community to identify the modes by which our person-of-new-type might produce complex sound for speech. The resonant chambers in her head were only good for amplification and modulation, not sound generation. The sub-team of specialists dedicated to this analysis had brilliantly concluded that, if anything, her people made sounds with a little flap of tissue over the windpipe, and their diagnosis was that this had somehow been irreparably damaged, perhaps by the intrusion of various items of medical equipment during her hospitalization.

None of these geniuses paid any mind to the messy clump of fibers in her throat just above that useless flapper. Obviously, the consensus ruled, those irregular shapes had something to do with directing food away from the air passage, or maybe they were for controlling infection, or perhaps it was nothing more than tissue overgrowth following some older injury.

They should have brought me into that discussion. Surely, anyone with half a brain would have noticed that the sounds she did produce emanated from those fibers: the groans, the cries of discomfort and distress—even the laughter. But those persons involved in the research possessed far too illustrious academic credentials to waste their efforts on actual observation. Vocalization is produced by the flexion of tissue in resonance chambers, not by some whistling effect of air blown over fibrous mats. That is simply obvious and natural. *Just how many useless images were produced of her skull?* I wondered.

No, it took Haillyen herself to produce the proper question, which was a simple one, directed to our own medical expert. "Just how, exactly, do people make the noises that they use to speak?"

I know the precise question because it was recorded on her flatscreen's memory. But I didn't see it for months, because it was Jemenga she asked, not me, and Jemenga has this unquenchable thirst for the dramatic approach. And once there was a clear diagnosis, his absolute faith that he could effect a cure was not only megalomaniacal, but also justified.

All the trips to town were better explained, now. The claim that Jemenga needed her input on an aspect of some paper or another always had seemed weak to me. But I had been quite ready to believe her bored of the isolated country life.

So, while I was imagining her taking in the delights of city life— enjoying the arts, the music … maybe even some modest stakes taking—Haillyen was engaged in a tedious sequence of medical procedures to reestablish lost nerve connections, followed by an even more tedious course of speech therapy. I know *that* because the speech therapist managed to extract a few publishable papers of her own out of the experience.

Meanwhile, the expedition preparations proceeded apace. We had a clearance from the publications police. We had a date on the calendar. We had a budget. We had a project plan—one that at least looked plausible. We had a team.

•    •    •

"We have a problem." Jemenga said. He was so pale onscreen, I reached for the controls to adjust the colors. He leaned in close to the camera and lowered his voice. "You need to get out."

# 13

*"Simply unbelievable. These conspirators harbored a fugitive alien, a creature teeming with infective microbes and horrific infestations, in the heart of our most pastoral, agriculturally sensitive region."*

- Insake Hailaware<br>Special Prosecutor

I STARED AT THE SCREEN and turned up the volume.

"Get out," Jemenga repeated, his voice even lower than before.

"Go out? Why?" I wondered. "Is there something in the weather report about an especially good sunset?"

Jemenga paused, took a breath, visibly calming himself, while his skin hues flickered from anxiety to anger. He spoke quickly and softly. "There's been a leak."

"A leak? What? There's been a toxic spill?"

True enough, if a disaster occurred, I'd be the last in the neighborhood to know. And Jemenga knew I never had the video on.

Jemenga twitched his fingers in dismissal, as if to say *No, no, not that kind of leak*, glanced from side to side as if looking for someone, and then said, absolutely humorlessly, "Hah, you caught me. Such a skilled jokester you are, old friend. Meet me at our old hangout downtown. You can help me work to improve my punchlines."

"Our old *hangout?*" I began, but then the serious grey of his expression sank in. *What hangout?* I puzzled. The only place we'd met recently that was even remotely "downtown" was the free clinic where Jemenga volunteered his copious free time … and where he'd extracted a hefty donation from my trust fund. To do that, I'd needed to get my aunts—the co-trustees—to assent. Abruptly, my mind shifted gears from Junior Scholar to Varayla Scion. *Oh. A leak. A dangerous leak.*

"Great idea," I said. "Shall I bring Auntie Adeleke's checkbook this time, too? And will you bring your sketchy little girlfriend?"

Jemenga forced a hollow-sounding laugh. "Oh, you bring all your most precious things and I'll bring mine," he said. "If you can pack seventy-nine articles into that old knapsack of yours, I'll spot you the first drink."

*What? Seventy-nine? Articles?* My mind raced. *No, he means Article Seventy-nine. From the Compact. 'In the event of incursion…'*

"So? Drinks and jokes?" Jemenga prompted. "Think fast … train arrives in an hour, if I remember the schedules right." I looked up, struggling to frame an appropriately cagey answer of my own, with the keywords of Article 79 rattling my thoughts. *Containment. Confinement. Sterilization.*

"Sure, Doctor J," I replied at long last, waving an exaggerated grin. "Keep the drinks flowing and the jokes clean. Very clean. Positively sterile. We need to respect the ladies, you know."

Jemenga sat back and looked at me appraisingly. He echoed my imitation of a drunken grin. "All righty, then. Best get your hefty mass out of that country cottage in a half-hour if you mean to make good on that promise."

"Indeed, I will," I said. "I was raised to make good on all my promises."

As the screen flicked to grey once more, I took a deep breath and gathered my thoughts.

*All my promises, aunties, yes, all of them.*

Collecting all my "precious things" took very little time. The work, of course, resided safely on my portable flatscreen and a backup pod small enough to slip into a pocket. Managing the residence of, first, a rambunctious child, and, later, a careless wastrel, the elder Varaylas had refrained from installing any of their art collection here. So, any precious items would be solely my own. The first thing stuffed into my "knapsack"—actually, the same oversized, tattered packbag

I'd hauled on the Expedition—was a paperboard box stuffed with old letters and a few photographs. Not mine. My parents'. My own little box of love-letters and keepsakes followed. Perhaps I was wasting my time on it, but that favorite childhood blanket did serve to pad the boxes. I hesitated at my library wall. Books were replaceable, no matter how attached I might be to my particular copies. I nearly turned away, but then reconsidered. *You're* not *going to burn* these, I thought furiously, and swept clean the shelf of poetry, twelve volumes into the bag. And because it was right there on the shelf above, staring at me forlornly, in went the plush kazeran that I'd carried with me day after day through my first year as an orphan.

*Enough*, I told myself. And I glanced at the clock. A quarter-hour gone. *Time to check the fuse-box.*

I've elided certain details about my aunts' country retreat. After all, most of these details were ones I myself was not intended to know. For example, when Haillyen and I stood in the driveway every week, chatting with the cart boy and feeding treats to his kazeran, we were at the exact spot my father had breathed his last. Of course, he'd earned that expiration by sending a half-dozen Treasury officers to a similar fate. The kitchen door by which I'd dashed out that day to apologize to the physical-therapy guru who'd led me to my ultimate career? My mother had pounded through that door herself, a repeating revolver in one hand and an early-model staser in the other. She failed to make it around the house to defend her husband. Had I not just that week begun school, at the little town primary-school that still operated just across the street from K'alare's library, I might have witnessed the bitter conclusions of their careers.

They should have run. Why they didn't angers me to this day. They were impulsive people, true, and prone to react with violence— at least according to court documents. But the home was a safe house—a Syndicate retreat. And it was built to run from. I knew this. I wasn't supposed to, but I've always been the kind of home-dweller who tinkers with the equipment, continually making little improvements. The nature of the fuse-box revealed itself to me during the first storm season for which I was at the house on my own.

Simply put, there was another utility box behind the fuse-box. And that utility box housed an entirely different category of *fuse*. The interior of that second box included a tidy circuit diagram and clear operating instructions, in case of emergency. Well, certain types of emergency.

Once I learned about the secondary fuse box, I conducted further investigations and subsequently conducted routine maintenance: timing devices, communicating wiring, detonators, sealed explosives. I'd always assumed my sole motivation was my compulsive need to be a good caretaker of the house my aunts had given me—while always wondering if they knew that I knew its complete history. How could they imagine I did not? Yet, why did they never discuss it? Had some mental therapist told them these layers of deception would somehow benefit me?

In that moment, reading through the self-destruct instruction sequence, carrying a packbag loaded with all of my most precious items, I understood.

This was still a safehouse. The Syndicate had made it so. And of course, my aunts knew I would discover the nature of the place. And that I would learn enough about my parents' errors to not emulate them in either the larger or the smaller details.

The road would have been easier, but I suspected the Sterilization team would take that approach, considering they would need to arrive with some heavy equipment. With timers activated, pausing only to snag a piece of fruit from the kitchen counter, I strolled quickly down the backyard slope and, for the last time, hopped over my favorite little stream. By the time I reached my neighbor's farm-track to town, the concussion-blast was only a distant thump, like the echo of a summer thunderstorm.

•　　　•　　　•

It was late, of course, by the time I arrived at Jemenga's little clinic. The whine of the fluorescent lights overhead grated on my nerves. I found Jemenga alone, slapping x-ray transparencies onto darkened viewing screens. I looked around for Haillyen.

"Is Haillyen here already?"

"Ssst. Sit. Listen. Think."

"Not my forte, Jemenga," I said, trying to sound jocular, while fighting back the imagined image of my sweet little house, with all of its secrets, crumbling to bits and bursting into flames.

"Right, Scholar Varayla. Look at these, here." And he flipped a switch to activate the nearest light board. He stretched out one dark arm, so his longest finger just touched the first image, the one on the right. "Don't ask how I got this; it's an original from Expedition One."

I leaned in to peer at the design. Fiddly dark traceries, glowing white shadows. What was it? Art? Scenery? I felt stupid. Again. "Cater to my ignorance a bit more, O Great One," I confessed, "Just what is this?"

He pulled a strongly-mimed double-take and eased my soul at last with his familiar rumbling laugh. "What was I expecting? It's a neural-activity scan, computer-enhanced. What does it look like to you?"

I was startled. "You mean this is someone's nervous system?" I looked closer. "It's just the brain, isn't it? I think I see it now; the outline is like the diagrams in my old anatomy textbook. But the picture I remember didn't look like this, not with those shiny squiggles. This reminds me of some of the corals you see in videos from the warmer seas near the equator, the fan-like ones. Is this some new kind of scan? What is it that the computer is enhancing?"

Jemenga let my questions run on and run dry. He just waited. The next image in his sequence was quite different. Again, the shadowy outline recalled the familiar curlicued egg of the cerebral cortex. But there was no fascinating design superimposed on it. Instead, I saw only an array of colorful blotches, more like a child's early art endeavor than the complex patterns of the first array.

"Well," I ventured. "This looks like another … um … brain scan, but without the interesting … er … artistic enhancement." And I hesitated, looking back and forth between the two. "Or is it that there's nothing to enhance in the second one? Is the second one defective or damaged, so it doesn't generate those designs?"

Still, Jemenga gestured me on to the third image, without interjecting any commentary, though his colors betrayed an inclination to swat some stupidity out of me. Very encouraging.

This last resembled the first. That is, there was the delicate tracery again, branching and re-branching, each new twiglet resembling its parent, and also echoing the whole, only on a progressively finer scale. Lit from behind, the design glowed as if infused with its own life.

I could only shrug. "All I can say is these are very pretty. They just don't mean anything to me."

Jemenga groaned and gave me his coldest, most serious glare. He reached out and flicked my left ear with his fingertips. "Listen here. How much of our award-winning paper have you actually read?"

I leaned back and tried to look huffy. But he was right, I had distanced myself somewhat from the medical content of that paper, styling myself as the skilled writer, not the medical expert. "Well, I'm not exactly a Skilled Physician, you know," I extemporized. "Can't claim to have followed all the details."

"What did you think of my conclusions regarding the foreign matter?"

"Foreign?"

"Yes, yes," he pressed on, his irritation rising, "the tendrils in the wound, the tissue that didn't match. What did you think kept the work restricted? Why do you think we slammed her into isolation so quickly?"

"Well …" I hesitated again.

The nights after the days I'd worked on those segments of the paper had been dream-filled nights, featuring continuous full-motion animations of twitching fibers, glowing wires snaking all over my house, demonic possession, and worse. But there had been all that follow-up material, the scans just before her hospital release that showed nothing. The paper concluded smugly that the alien tissue incursion had been completely absorbed and defeated by the native tissue.

Jemenga leaned close. "What do you think it is?" His eyes loomed large and shimmered with intensity. "The foreign matter? An experimental error or something real?"

I couldn't help shuddering. "Oh, it was real enough. I saw it. I all but touched it. But you said it was gone. What does it matter? Is some stupid official refusing you a Staffing Release Form?"

There was some comfort in identifying a problem that I *could* solve. Surely that was that all there was to it. My mind swiftly recast its routing to the political connections that had been so useful in the past.

"What does it *matter*? Ansegwe, when I read your work, I can manage to forget briefly that you are still a vapid, ignorant naïf!"

I had to get a little angry at that. You understand. I thumped his table. Just a little. It was entirely his fault that the drink sloshed on the folders stacked there. I flinched, anticipating an explosion.

But as ever, Jemenga retained his sense of humor. He merely laughed at me, called me a juvenile wastrel, mopped off the topmost item and handed it to me. "My fault. Blame me. I should have given you this long ago. But there was that problem you were having last year. You were already scared, over-anxious. And then we all got to working."

I stood staring at the folder, a smear of orange darkening its cover. That cover was thoroughly decorated, warning that the information contained therein was Highly Confidential, Security Restricted, For Official Use Only. "Are you sure? I don't have any kind of security clearances."

"I do." That gave me pause. Just how long had Jemenga had this thing? And what about *his* political connections? How far did they extend? "What is it?"

"Read it. You'll see. It's self-explanatory." And he reached out with those impressively muscular dark tentacles and pushed me firmly onto the nearest seat. I opened the report and fell into my nightmares.

# 14

*"Transfer Group 1.1: no survivors. Group 1.2: no survivors. Group 1.3: one incapacitated, two deceased. Group 1.4: two incapacitated, one deceased. One incapacitated from 1.3 returned. Group 1.5 (armored): two deceased on-site, one incapacitated, one bifurcation in transfer point closure, retrieved three units (one set of recovered remains from Group 1.3, two incapacitated in 1.3 returned). Group 1.6: ordered to stand down."*

– Transfer Project: Expedition One
Controlled Document TR-A5973.57.U1-Closed

I'D EXPECTED A STERILE, heavily-redacted report—one of those documents in which most of the content has been obliterated. For instance, my parents' criminal records are all but impossible to puzzle out. Instead, here I found page after page of clear, vivid, reporting; every word intact; every connotative indicator mark plainly revealing the emotional state of the author. He or she— there was no attribution—wrote like a first-hand witness to the utter debacle that was Expedition One.

So, what was this new universe like—the one they dubbed "Wide Plains Universe"—based on the peaceful, open plain to which Transfer Point #57 provided access for the translation engineers? The report opened with initial imaging from robotic explorers, showing Wide Plains to be a lovely, pastoral paradise, where slow-moving herbivores nibbled their way through masses of grey-green vegetation, harried on occasion by small, furry predators.

But in the next section, the report moved on to the first mission with people. Then, everything changed. Herbivores and carnivores alike vanished from the scene, replaced by ghastly demons plummeting out of the sky. Their light-emitting eyes glimmered like precious jewels as laser-like beams sought out and fixed upon their targets. The smells alone were awful—blood, fear pheromones, vomit … and worse. Even as weapons were reached for—weapons only brought along to ward off those little furry predators—wide wings snapped open, enfolding their victims. Jaws gaped, tongues like razors lanced into skulls, and brains became infected with nightmare patterns of light.

I had to pause.

"Wait," I said. "Jemenga?"

"What?"

"This must have been written much later, after some of the people recovered."

"Nobody recovered." His voice was grim.

"Then how—"

"There were recordings. Cameras. They sent in a robot, later, to retrieve the cameras. And the bodies."

"But the detail, there's more here than cameras would tell."

He shrugged. "Imagine being tasked with writing this narrative." Unstated, but clear: *Consider that person's need to fill in the missing details, to be sure no one would try this again.*

I pressed on. "How could it have gone so far? Affected so many people? Surely, after the first group was struck down, there wouldn't have been a go-ahead signal."

Even on our journey to the so-called Deep Valley universe, where we'd found Haillyen, the second group wasn't allowed to walk through until the first group sent back the properly coded "safe to proceed" message.

"How do you think that rule got started? They were just going on all the good data they got from the robots. If you read through all the technical material in there, you'll see they were much more focused on the shift constraints—the way transfer point lifetimes allow only a few to translate through each time, and the way you have to wait a while between transfer-point opportunities."

"So, you're telling me they didn't even have a clue something was wrong?"

"Well," he said, gesturing to the folder. "If you get that far, you'll see that one who wasn't killed outright managed to wander back through during Group 1.4's shift."

I looked down and flipped pages to that point. *Oh. Oh, my.*

I took a deep breath, and resolutely closed the folder. *No more.* I let my fingers trace around its edges as if that could seal the information safely within, and I sat back to let the flushing shades of anguish drain a little.

I forced myself to look up once more, seeing Jemenga's row of brain-scan images in a new light.

"Gods, gods," I murmured. "So, this is what she escaped from." A sudden pang struck me. "If I hadn't stood out there in the open … If I hadn't gone back …" No wonder she hadn't wanted to talk about it.

"We can't be sure it's the same thing. Expedition One was shut down twelve years ago now. That's about ten years before the rest of us even heard about these alternate universes."

"But surely that's what you're thinking? That somehow these creatures also dwell in Haillyen's universe?" I asked hesitantly.

Jemenga looked drained too, his colors mixed and fluxing. He shrugged thoughtfully. "Or that somehow Haillyen wandered into theirs. Transfer points are everywhere, so they say."

I wondered how he'd brought himself to join our Expedition, knowing the possibilities.

Then a cold thought forced its way to the surface: *Of course. Jemenga saw this information before we even checked in at our transfer point. He* knew *about this.*

"So," I said. "When you heard about this, you signed up for the latest expedition. You were going to collect and dissect one of these monsters. You were going to get your Kalinidor Prize by solving the mystery of Expedition One." *No wonder the pastoral beauty of the Deep Valley wilderness didn't impress Jemenga—he was too busy looking for laser-eyed brain-eaters.*

I felt the deep, churning blues of righteous rage lighting my face. "You knew what it was, right there in the forest, didn't you? Why keep it from me?" I demanded. "Up until then, it could have stayed your secret. But at that point, it was my right, as family, to know the facts. Why didn't you *tell* me?

"Was it because no one would give you clearance to send her back if they'd suspected anything? You just wanted to be able to get her under all your precious *scanners*, Jemenga!"

"What are you saying?" he said. His eyes were wide and deep, his colors slightly grey, with touches of rose. "I had no idea what we were seeing! Only that it was more than strange anatomy and a stroke!" He stood, regaining his size advantage.

"Don't try to lead me on. I remember that day perfectly," I retorted. "You let it slip—you told me it reminded you of something. You said you'd have to 'look it up'. You didn't need to look up anything." I shook the folder at him. "You *knew*."

Jemenga flicked out one arm and snatched the documents out of my grasp. But then he simply leaned back, coiled his fingers around the edge of the folder, and regarded me with something like caution. I could feel the old anger simmering down deep; my fingers twitched involuntarily.

Jemenga took a breath, and said, quietly, "What would make you believe I hadn't seen this report, Ansegwe? And, even if I had, how could it have changed how I treated her? Haillyen's case didn't match the profile."

True. Haillyen's jabbering may have sounded strange to us, but it was speech all the same. And while it may have been crazy, in the colloquial sense, for her to appeal to a party of alien intruders for help, clearly Haillyen was sane—daring perhaps—but sane all the same. It was the stroke that had been so debilitating. And she had recovered, unlike any of the crew of Expedition One.

I wondered, *Are they all dead by now? Or are the four insane ones still locked away somewhere?*

Jemenga pressed on. "And she was my patient. Why would I lie to a patient? What good does that ever do?"

"All that extra time in your hospital," I pointed out.

He waved that off. "Yes, yes, of course. We had to study her condition thoroughly. There was not much time. The alien tissue degenerated quickly. We extracted what we could, isolated it, studied it."

I continued to glare at him, struggling to gather thoughts out of my anger. "And what do you have to report from those studies?" I asked, finally.

"We can't make a full report. The Reportage Police won't let us. They don't need to say why. In fact, explanations are just as likely to violate security regulations. Or so I gather. Don't you see?

"That's why I went off scrounging for that thing I so vaguely remembered." Jemenga sat down with a thump. I spared a little energy from glaring to simply look at him. He was tired, exhausted, sagging. "And you think I've been playing a game with you all this time."

"Obviously," I said, and my fingers gestured disdain and regret and betrayal. I couldn't stop them any more than I could shift my colors.

Jemenga stretched his arms out to their full length and grunted heavily. Instinctively, my muscles braced as if for a physical attack. But though his own body rippled with strength, it was only words that he brandished. "This is no game, junior woodsman. It's just taken me most of this past year to track down this information."

"Oh, yes, of course it did."

"Yes," and his own gestures were curt, irritated by my sarcasm. "There *was* something familiar about the strange fibers. It took ages to remember just what they reminded me of. And then, it was not something real, just a fiction."

"A what?"

"A piece of writing positing a what-if scenario, for amusement."

I really didn't have time for this kind of nonsense, and I'm sure my own irritation was clearly limned on my face. "What amusement is that? Another pretentious advance in artistic prevarication? Does it call for the talents of actors with better control over their autonomous responses than the idiots in the video serials?"

"Don't sneer. You know perfectly well, from working with Haillyen, that properly punctuated text does accurately report words, feelings, and detail gestures in a compact form."

"And what did this *fiction* have to do with our *friend*?"

Jemenga stretched out again, this time to finger over the neatly ordered material on his desk. From the far corner, he retrieved a thin booklet in cheap, yellowed paper. "Here," he said. "Be gentle; it's old. Won't hold up to abuse."

The paper crackled as I turned pages. Its condition added verisimilitude to Jemenga's claim. The booklet contained more than one such *fiction*, but Jemenga's selection was easily located: it was fronted by an illustration that matched in eerie detail the scans glowing before us.

Jemenga leaned over a little, as I studied that picture. "It was the artist, you see," he said. "I spent months tracking down the author, only to learn that she'd got the idea from this artistic boyfriend she'd had at the time. Amateur artist. Professional Nurse."

It seems this nurse had been part of the medical team called in after the Expedition One disaster. They were all pledged to secrecy, but the artistic impulse combined with certain confidences in the course of romance became a failure in the security screen.

And hence this little what-if tale, wherein the intrepid explorer uses a magical transport to reach a land inhabited by drifting, fanged monsters that suck his mind out of his brain. The piece was short, but vividly drawn. A promotional blurb on the cover described the work as a "metaphorical excursion into the unexplored universe of interpersonal relationship anxiety."

Jemenga's famous self-confidence reasserted itself. "You see, don't you? The problem? This trip back. There are decisions to make. We can't delay."

I was impatient by now, the threads of the conversation twisting in my mind. "As I said at the start, what difference does it make when you knew already? It says right there in our paper there's no problem . . . no remaining *alien tissue*." How I hated those words.

"Yes, yes. It *says* right there." He clicked his jaw disdainfully and countered his words with a wry gesture.

All I could say was, "Oh." The extended applications for "*fiction*" were beginning to take shape in my mind. And how new an idea was it anyway? Hadn't my old school chums been enviably adept at convincing their parents to write those notes of excuse?

My eyes were drawn inescapably back to the third scan image. The one that was fundamentally different. The one with the odd shape. It was more of a half-ovoid than an egg. Smaller, too. But not a child. Nor a person with a poorly-developed or damaged cortex. The shape was whole and smooth, crinkled with the familiar convolutions of brain tissue.

Meanwhile, the alien web superimposed on the ovoid's surface glowed ominously under the image-viewing lamps.

"This is Haillyen's, isn't it?" I said, and my fingers trembled. The date was clearly printed on each scan. This was no two-year-old examination. It was dated yesterday.

# 15

*"Yes, the result of the effort to conduct sterilization proceedings at the country site was an embarrassment. And no, the affair at the free clinic is not what I would consider the highlight of my career."*

– Elesennen Haileski
Chief of Operations, Security Directorate

MY FINGERS QUIVERED as I traced the date on that recent scan, the filigree of shadows cast by the lightbox twisting across my skin. "It grew back. It's like it was never gone."

Jemenga reached out and snatched the image from the display. "Yes, yes. Finally, you see my dilemma. This image must be destroyed. The authorities cannot know there was anything but a failed scan attempt." His arms twisted with the anguish of a frustrated scientist. "But if I destroy it, then how can I study it? And how do we explain the cancellation?"

"Cancellation? Of what?" I turned to stare at him puzzledly.

It was Jemenga's turn to thump the table. This time, the cup that before had merely sloshed over rebounded into the air and toppled on its side. He ignored the sweet liquid flowing off the edge of the table to spatter the floor. Instead, he slapped one arm around my shoulders and leaned in until his face filled my field of view.

"Think!" he commanded. "There is no question now of this excursion we'd planned! I'm not sending Haillyen off alone into those unforgiving woods with nothing but a text recorder and a brain full of alien neural matter!"

His gestures flashed in front of my eyes like birds of prey. I jerked back, startled, all of the consequences and conflicts tumbling through my mind at once. An irrational impulse to flee flooded my system. Fighting it down left me queasy and dizzy.

As usual, Jemenga was absolutely right, through and through. What if he *had* told me all this when he'd come that night last year? I remembered now, the packet of papers he'd hastily thrust back into his bag without even mentioning them. How well would I have slept, then, with actual facts and figures to add realism to my nightmares?

Watching the colors of my emotions flow, Jemenga echoed my thoughts. Softly, but in a rambling tone as if that would keep me calm, he said, "I meant to spare you worry. It was only a recheck, that first time I managed to prise her out of your protective keeping. It had been months since her last, perfectly clear, scan. But the scan showed a trace of something, something that might have been a data flaw. So, I scheduled another. Even then, it could have been a vestige that we'd missed before—and, for the longest time, that anomaly was stable. But then it just … exploded."

My ears twitched in reaction, recalling the morning's distant thunder. "Exploded. Yes. I see," I said, trying for a light tone.

"I have a theory," Jemenga went on, "that it has to do with verbal language acquisition, but the evidence is shaky."

When the door shook under a barrage of raps, both of us jerked to attention and turned as one. The door latch rattled as if someone were struggling with the lock, but finally it unlatched with a snap, and the door swung inward.

Haillyen poked her face around the door. "Sorry. Handle made for you people," she apologized.

Then she spotted the displays on the lightbox and strode into the room. She folded her arms in that impossibly angular way and stared at the images thoughtfully. When she extended one arm and traced a stubby finger along the webwork in the old images, I couldn't help cringing.

But when Haillyen finally turned away from the scans, there was no sign of distress. "So beautiful!" she exclaimed. "Just like dreams!"

Somehow, I managed to stay calm. What to say? I had made the same mistake. "It's not what you think, Haillyen," I said, knowing I could not keep the sadness out of my face. Her face became still, her eyes moving from mine to Jemenga's.

"What?" she asked. "Why so unhappy?"

"It's not just pretty lines," I managed. But there I stopped short, my fingers tangled in contradictions.

"Where's mine?" She turned to Jemenga and laughed. "There it is!" She dodged lightly between us, snatched the sheet from his grasp, and snapped it in place next to the others. "Mine is the best, isn't it?" She turned back to the display and spread her awkward array of fingers across the tracery of the invader in her own brain.

"You are right, not just pretty lines." Her voice had that rough quality I'd been anticipating, but with her free hand, she deliberately sketched a quick series of delighted smiles. "He is here." She tipped her feet up to reach just a little higher, leaned her face close to the image and lightly pressed her mouth against it. "Az-dyel, my dear. I am coming soon."

Then she turned briskly back to the pair of us, our arms frozen in the midst of argument, our colors confused. My normally talkative fingers struggled to smile calmly, while I fumbled for words. Jemenga came up with only the obvious, "Whatever are you talking about, Haillyen? What do you imagine these pictures show?"

She rolled the dark centers of her eyes up under her eyelids, a gesture I'd never quite managed to interpret, and pulled the flatscreen out of her satchel. "This needs better detail than my talking can give you, I think." She scribbled hastily, while shifting her position so that we could both focus on her words. "This picture we have here is just my brain, with my friend Az-dyel's—" She paused, searching for the right word. "Let's say, his *network* is superimposed on it. I am very relieved, after all those annoying scans, that Jemenga has confirmed that once I find Az-dyel, we will still be able to talk. Why does this trouble you so? I can see from these other pictures that your people have met ones like Az-dyel before."

"But this woman," I stammered out, jerking one tentacle out far enough to tap the right-most scan. "This woman here is insane."

"Not anymore," Jemenga added helpfully. "She's dead."

"Oh? Was she very old then? Or ill?" Haillyen asked. Perhaps, I wondered dizzily, close contact with me had rendered Haillyen as densely naïve as me.

As if acting on their own, Jemenga's arms reached out and his grasping fingers fastened on her bony shoulder joints. "People like your friend killed her. They all died, all of our people who met those monsters."

On *killed* and *died*, his arms jerked. I could hear Haillyen's teeth clacking together. The flatscreen clattered to the floor. Haillyen wrenched herself free and retreated to the far corner of the room.

"Essplain!" she cried. "Az-dyel kill no people. I know. This … this network …" and she waved towards the silvery net of alien growth. "It is for talk. Not kill. Talk. *Talk.*" And all our talk ceased.

Together, the three of us stared at the mute argument of the Expedition One scans. The now-familiar sensation of a shift in perception stole over my mind.

"Jemenga," I ventured. "When you make a scan like this, how do you get the image out of the machine? How do you save it? Or share it with another doctor?"

Jemenga grunted. He seemed not to be listening. I looked over at Haillyen, still leaning against the far wall, her attitude that of mingled caution and distress. That annoying fluid was flowing freely down her face again. And me with no drying cloths handy.

"Haillyen," I said, trying to keep the quaver out of my gestures, "it's all right. We'll sort this out. It's—"

"Wires," Jemenga announced. "The information is sent on wires. The machines talk to each other on a *network* of wires."

"And if I take a machine from, say, Quazwallade, and put wires from one of our machines into that, what happens?"

Jemenga shook his fingertips. "Nothing much. We have compatible systems. But something from Terende, now. I had a burn patient once, because of the voltage difference." He surged forward, snatched up a keypad from his desk and began hammering on it. More scans snapped up on the display screen beside the lightbox, a rapid-fire sequence of images like the first one, brains infected with shimmering networks of alienness.

Those familiar hues of eager curiosity flooded across Jemenga's features. He stared at his array of images, rearranging them furiously, muttering fiercely to himself. Then he broke off, looking back and forth at the pair of us watching him.

"Yes. Yes, I can see it. I just can't believe it. They were trying to communicate? But our systems were incompatible?" He stretched to pick up the old report and began paging through the awful sequence once more.

When noise echoed in the hallway, shouted commands from the waiting room out front, Jemenga didn't even look up. I took a deep breath and shook off the contemplative mood.

"Haillyen," I said. "Quickly, go and lock the door." She started to question the order, but took one look at my face and hurried to fulfill it. Pausing briefly at the door, she also turned off the overhead light, leaving the room illuminated only by the lightbox.

"What's wrong?" she asked, very quietly.

"Let's just say Jemenga and I aren't the only ones who misinterpreted those scans," I said, keeping my voice low as well. I scooped her flatscreen off the floor and handed it to her. "Can you send a message to K'alare for me? Ask her to meet us at my Uncle Eskewere's place—and tell her to pack her gear for the trip, that the schedule's been moved up on our travel."

She gave me another of her uninterpretable expressions, but bent over the screen and typed furiously. In the meantime, I shouldered Jemenga aside and retrieved all of the scan images, stuffing them into the folder with the old report.

"What's your problem, Ansegwe?" he protested, flushing angrily and reaching for the folder.

Holding the precious contraband just out of reach, I stretched for a way to break his focus. "Jemenga, remember this morning, when you called my house? What did you tell me then?"

He paused, and looked around the darkened room. "Have you already forgotten?" he said. "I told you to get out."

"Yes, and now *we* need to get out. Now. Listen." Muffled voices rumbled somewhere in the empty clinic. An earsplitting crash at the end of the nearest hallway announced the breach of the security door that normally protected only patients' privacy. We all stared at the door Haillyen had just locked, as if it were about to shatter.

"Now, old man," I said. "Where's your secret way out when

you need to dodge one of the overly affectionate dowager donors who fund this place?"

Jemenga grinned with both hands. "Ah," he said. "So, you do listen to my stories, after all.

"This way."

# 16

*"The multiverse is winking at us. It's as if there is some deep inside secret about reality, a joke that we're just not getting, but that we'd better catch on to if we want to survive."*

– Kinsala Tkerelon
Chancellor, Cignali University

WITHOUT A BACKWARD GLANCE, Jemenga led us from the diagnostic room to an adjoining laboratory space, which connected via a narrow corridor to a series of treatment rooms—each quietly waiting for the next day's round of patients. The last of these had a second door, which opened to an emergency-exit hallway. Jemenga slid a coded card-key across the doorway's sensor, and held us back until the blue warning light shifted to a welcoming gold.

"All right," Jemenga gestured. "The exit won't sound an alarm now."

In seconds, we were safely out of sight of the clinic, and not long after we were tucking into a complimentary dinner at a pub owned by an old friend. During my secondary-school days, weekends at "Uncle" Eskewere's estate had been a welcome relief from long, dull weeks attempting to satisfy the scholastic expectations of my aunts. He'd been a close confidant of my father's, and often spoke regretfully of him—not for deeds performed, but for the failure to attend to the risks those deeds presented.

At any rate, the odds of the barman making a surreptitious call to the police were less than those of the average householder returning home from Eskewere's casino with more than half the funds he'd arrived with.

"All well and good," Jemenga was saying, feigning fastidious reluctance as he snagged yet another portion of deep-fried fish from the steaming pan at the center of the table. "How are you expecting to dance into the Transfer Project center with a proscribed alien creature and a collection of, well, fugitives?"

"I suppose," I began, "I'm hoping we can benefit from what they call The Element of Surprise."

"Hmm?"

"He means," Haillyen cut in, "if we are running away, they won't think we'll run towards …" Short on verbal vocabulary, she gestured for me to go on.

"Yes, right," I said. "They'll assume we're headed to a hideout of some kind."

Jemenga laughed and scooped another serving of vegetables onto his plate. "If so, are we surprising them yet?" Then he looked up, rumbled another laugh, and waved towards the door of the banquet room we were occupying. "Welcome!" he called out.

Haillyen shushed him and appealed to me for help.

I followed Jemenga's gaze and laughed myself. "It's all right, Haillyen," I said. "It's K'alare, here at last. Excuse me."

Jemenga covered his eyes in mock horror as I scrambled to my feet and hurried to embrace my love at the door. A moment ago, I'd been only claiming everything would be all right. Now, I felt sure it would be so.

•　　　•　　　•

On the surface, it seemed so simple: we'd just turn up at the TransComm complex, convince the crew that our already-approved trip had been rescheduled, and slip Haillyen into the walk-through at the last moment. We argued over several approaches to the deception, until K'alare finally broke into the conversation.

"Think about the kind of people you're trying to fool," she said. "You're talking about engineers, scientists. These are people who are skeptical by nature."

"You're saying we should just give up?" Jemenga said.

"No, no," she said. "I'm saying you should use a different approach. Think about it. What motivates them? What do they care about? What do you have in common with them?" She'd leaned over the table with an inclusive gesture that reminded me how the other members of my own expedition team worked together—sometimes to ridicule me—but at other times …

"I'm not sure I can explain this the right way," I started, and K'alare waggled her fingers with an encouraging *go ahead*. "But aren't scientists basically explorers? Aren't they after some kind of truth about the universe?"

"Yes," she prompted. "So?"

"So, you mean—"

"Yes, my dear Ans'we."

"You're serious. Just tell them the truth?" I know I was every shade of skeptical myself, at that moment.

"Well, not just 'the truth'. Tell them of your discovery. That this universe where all the people died is the home of an alien race that wants to talk to them. And then—What's wrong, Haillyen?"

Haillyen was waving her hand in the air.

"It's OK, K'alare," I said. It's their gesture for 'Let me speak.'"

"Thanks," said Haillyen. "You talk fast. Hard to join in. But there is more. I can share knowledge Az-dyel gave me, about the walking between worlds, how it works, why it works—or doesn't work—the way it does."

Our little circle sat in silence and stared at her, then. She stared back, and finally tried a hesitant gesture of *all right?* And said, hesitantly, "Did I say something wrong?"

Jemenga broke out his most winning grin. "Well. You've been carrying the price of our passage around in that hairy little skull of yours all the time," he rumbled. "There is no better bribe we can offer than answers to their questions about this Translation business."

"Just don't call it a bribe," K'alare cautioned. "You'll insult them. Just bring them the knowledge. They'll know what needs done."

•    •    •

After an uncomfortable night attempting to sleep on the floor of a dining room after pub closing, and a long ride in the windowless cargo bay of a transport truck, we were none of us up to par on arrival at TransComm. Once we'd talked our way through to the project engineers, the experience for Haillyen became daunting, as she stood peppered with questions from a ring of eager researchers. They had linked her flatscreen to a larger display, which opened up the circle somewhat.

"So, you've been to Wide Plains Universe and escaped unhurt?" was the most incredulous query—with a most unexpected response.

"Not exactly. Az-dyel had travelled to … what do you call it? Deep Valley? And from there to my home universe. They're all connected, you know."

"Oh, so your culture has translation engineering, too?"

Again. "Not exactly. Sometimes the … transfer points … they can let one of Az-dyel's people through."

This was not the sort of news they were looking for.

"But once he comes to a place like Deep Valley, Az-dyel cannot fly. He needs help. The same for here and for my home. We all have too much gravity."

I felt the relief flow through the room like a warm wave. But at that point, one of the engineers pointed out that time was running short. The scientists set aside any anxieties about scary monsters popping freely through random transfer points in what they had already started calling the Translation Network. They focused on dragging out of Haillyen every little nugget about inter-universe connectivity and transport that she'd been able to glean. Their excitement was palpable. Everyone was taking notes; one of the fellows was sketching diagrams as if his life depended on it. I began to wonder if they'd change their minds and make her stay just to extend the interview.

At last, though, the questions began to repeat and Haillyen's answers devolved to a sequence of "That's just another way of seeing the connections that I told you about five minutes ago." Haillyen set down her stylus and flexed her fingers.

"I think I've sprained my whole hand," she said, though sketching a smile to soften the complaint.

"We're nearly ready for you," the lead engineer said from across the room.

K'alare had been watching her plan unfold from an unused workstation in a quiet corner. She spoke up at that point. "What do we need to do?" she said. "Neither Haillyen nor I have done this before."

I'd forgotten. Haillyen had been unconscious at the time—and from the sound of it, her prior experience with translation hadn't needed our kind of equipment. One of the younger engineers—a student like myself, maybe—stepped forward eagerly. I leaned a bit to the side to see her name badge: Ensense Halense.

"K'alare," I whispered. "Look. You have a cousin on the team."

"Over there," my future cousin-in-law was saying, "above that blue platform with the cables running all around it, at certain predictable times there is a stable transfer point that leads to Deep Valley. You can't see it, but—"

Haillyen interrupted her. "Right. The connection points are very tiny. But Az-dyel can see them," she volunteered.

"Pity he's not here then," the young engineer said, without a trace of irony. "He could help us spot new transfer points. You wouldn't believe all the steps we have to go through to find, validate, test, and preview a possible transfer point. Not to mention correlating which ones go to different locations, but to a common universe." She sighed wistfully, clearly longing for a handy brain-invading monster to eliminate all that work.

"Anyhow," she went on, "the monitoring system—" a bank of computers with displays showing scrolling figures and graphical readouts "— lets us know the transfer point is in range. Well, we call it 'range', but it's more of a time thing. Do I need to explain that?"

"No, please skip the details for me," K'alare said. "And I think our travel partner has enough details in her head already."

Halense smiled that self-effacing smile that engineers lean towards. "I understand. Cut through the jibber-jabber. Once the point's in range, we fire up the translation engines, which widen the transfer point enough for us to send a few people through. You'll see a blue fuzzy tunnel appear on that platform. And you'll have about five minutes for everyone in your party to walk through."

"Oh, that short a time?"

"Yes. There are alarms that sound. Don't let them frighten you; they're just to keep people moving. If you run out of time, well, then, you just wait for the next time the transfer point's in range. This one's great: it loops around every thirty minutes or so."

I held my breath for just a second, waiting to see if either K'alare or Haillyen would ask The Question. But it was Jemenga who did it, purely out of mischief, since he knew the answer.

"So, does anyone ever get cut in half because the transfer point closed?"

And she gave him the official, stock answer: "No, no, of course not. Never. That's what all the monitors and alarms are for."

The words in the Expedition One personnel report echoed in my mind, but I refrained from sharing that news. Surely this eager, well-trained intern didn't need to hear of that "one bifurcation" from so many years ago. Still, I'll confess, I was more anxious during my third walk through a transfer point than I was either of the first two times.

•     •     •

The four of us stepped out on the other side and met the base-camp greeting staff as usual. Each of us fidgeted nervously with our overloaded packs of gear while we worked through the anticipated questions about our project. At last we set off at a strong marching pace, bypassing Base Camp itself, directly to the little lake where I still remembered cooling my blistered feet so long ago.

There, K'alare and Jemenga set up our Expeditionary Station. The project statement claimed important biological data could be obtained from this tiny seasonal pool. Jemenga himself had little interest in microscopic biota, and had written into the prospectus some "essential" collecting of his own. He had developed a passionate interest in better understanding the furry-tailed rodents that had expressed such intelligent interest in our campsites. His pack was loaded with auto-triggered camera gear, radio-tagging equipment, and collapsible traps.

"As for bait," he explained, for K'alare's benefit, "all we'll need is a portion of any of our own rations. The little beasts eat everything."

K'alare may have worked as a librarian, but she'd trained for museum work. During planning, she'd welcomed the chance to take an active role in something that could end up in a collection she might curate in the future. With elaborate care, she unpacked the sample vials and labels she needed, and endured one more round of instruction from Jemenga.

Meanwhile, my own concern centered on Haillyen. She needed to be well off on her way into forbidden territory before any inspectors wandered up the trail from base camp to check on our adherence to plan. Together, we re-sorted items from the group's bags to stock her custom-made pack with everything she might need on her journey. The challenge was to winnow her load to make sure it was manageable for her.

"That's enough fiddling," she said, finally. "Look at the sun. I need to get moving." She hefted the pack and adjusted the straps one more time.

I hefted mine in turn. "All right, then. Let's go."

She paused, looking down deliberately. "Ansegwe," she sighed. "I already told you no."

# 17

*"The guiding principle of my work has been to share my own recurring epiphanies of how our preconceptions lead us astray. Any child may learn the trick of finding the cool part of a flame, to amaze friends by placing a fragile manipulative finger in the fire. The small warrior applies strength and resilience not evident from mere size, to overcome an opponent relying on mass and weaponry. We fail ourselves when we approach the strange with fear and trepidation, not realizing our own alien natures."*

– Varayla Ansegwe
Poet Laureate

I'D KNOWN HAILLYEN would object to my company, so I'd come prepared with a formal argument. "I know you're worried about being observed leaving the approved research zone, but let's be realistic: the only likely observers are animals. The base camp staff are not at all interested in spying on us—nor do they have time for it."

She crossed her arms and glowered at me. I think. She didn't have the right colors, but her overall attitude conveyed a familiar annoyance with me.

"Also, the researchers who reported the existence of some kind of people had come back from a very long trip down out of the mountains, and didn't you tell me that the Stick Men who assaulted you were explorers themselves? So, that means we don't really need to worry about exposing my horrifying scary monster-ness and frightening the native people."

She looked up at me with those bright eyes brimming, and I congratulated myself for winning her over by making fun of myself.

"All right," she relented. "But only as far as the top of the cliff trail."

Apparently, my logical reasoning and humor had been insufficient. However, she was smart enough to accept the offer of having a hiking partner willing to carry her baggage up the fierce zig-zags of the trail from the valley floor to the high plateau.

Finally, though, we reached the top of that trail, and Haillyen insisted on reclaiming her pack. We had been in the midst of a conversation of some interest, so we trudged on together for a space. Well, make that for the rest of the morning. Finally, we came to a little trickle of a stream, and we stopped. I glanced around, and to my astonishment I recognized the place.

"Look!" I exclaimed. "It's our last camp!"

"Oh, really?" she said, turning to see my hues of pleasure and surprise.

But she did not argue; there was nothing to challenge. Our fire pit was obvious; no one had taken the time to dismantle it, and even if someone had tried, the signs of burning were still discernible. I even snagged a scrap of some plastic litter that was peeking out from under a rock.

"Here," I said. "A souvenir for Alekwa. She can use this to lecture her next team about tidiness."

"I remember reading something," she said. "A long time ago. I remember they said the mountains were fragile. It seemed incredible, like so many things that grown-ups claim. I didn't believe it at all. I wonder how long this campsite will be here?"

I stood silent, listening to the strangely familiar, raucous birds in the trees overhead. The sun warmed us with its golden light and, undoubtedly, less-appealing wavelengths were damaging our skin, but the breeze was chilly. I had begun composing a poem on the scenery, and now it began to be one about protecting the beauty of the wilderness.

"Haillyen?" I asked. "Did those grown-ups of long ago have ideas on the right way to travel in places like this?"

She sighed. By now, I understood the wetness in her tone, the incipient sadness. Yet she answered, "Yes, but I was not one of those who listened. Besides, I'm sure you will find better ways on your own." Then she, too, stared curiously around the campsite. "You know, Ansegwe, I don't remember this place at all. That was when I was … was ill, wasn't it?"

"Yes, that's right. I'm sorry. How could I have forgotten?" I apologized.

She brushed off the teardrops with one hand and waved a weak little smile with the other. "Don't be sorry. Be happy. I was so far gone. I am still so amazed and grateful and happy that you brought me through that."

"Well … I couldn't … it was … you were … I mean … Haillyen?"

What a relief that Jemenga had refrained from coming with us. He would have laughed seeing me at such a loss for words. But Haillyen merely leaned close to me, twined her fingers in mine, and gave me one of her own soft, musical laughs.

"I have a gift for you, Varayla Ansegwe," she said, nearly solemn, looking up into my colorful eyes with her tiny dark ones. I waited, wondering.

She took a deep breath, and spoke clearly, "It is time you knew my name."

"What?"

"Have you also forgotten that you named me Haillyen?" She laughed at my expression. "Well, I remember. I was so frightened at the time, and it was so funny, I couldn't help but accept it. Somehow, it made everything else bearable. Whenever all the changes and strangeness became too much for me, I could just say to myself, 'I am Haillyen' and make myself laugh inside."

"What do you mean?" I wasn't sure whether to be insulted or confused. And I knew perfectly well that she could read that combination of responses as well as I could read a dissertation.

"Now, don't be insulted." (What did I tell you?) She even stretched one arm across my back and gently smoothed down my spines. "Calm down, silly. Just think back. Remember. I had been saying something to you, over and over, something that sounded like that. You guessed it was my name. I liked it. I kept it that way. But it's about time you found out why."

I still felt a little huffy. "Why? What does it matter? It doesn't matter to me if you really didn't mind me calling you the wrong name for two whole years."

She made that twitchy jerk of her shoulder bones that passed for a shrug. "Here, hand over that ancient comp of yours."

"What? I thought you'd decided you could only adequately conceal one technological device."

"Just for a minute, Ansegwe. Please? Or do I have to *smile* at you?" And she paired a proper smile with her own bizarre tooth-baring gesture. I leaned back in mock terror, wishing I could adjust my tints to match the gesture.

"I surrender," I said, handing over the battered notepad.

Deft and sure now, she stabbed the stylus at the screen until she retrieved that ancient file of our first comp conversation. Thanks to my well-established history as a compulsive data keeper, in no time we were viewing her first effort to write in a set of letters from her own language.

"Drat," I complained. "We still have work to do. I want the rest of that writing system."

"Sorry, my dear," she said. "Too late now. But look. This, right here, this is my name, the name my parents gave me anyway. It can be our little secret."

I stared at the little screen, reeling once more under that eerie sensation of *I've completely misunderstood*. I recognized the series, "Bar with a bar on top, Hai ... loop with a stem, ll ... couple of bumps, ye ... but then there's another loop—"

She interrupted, reading off the names of her alien letters. "We call them *tee*, *ay*, and *em*. You see the *ay* repeats at the end. It's a lot like your writing, but without the emotive accenting. All phonetic, though we evolved multiple ways to spell the same sounds. But that's my original name: Tama." She giggled a little, adding, "No finger waves to go with it."

She turned thoughtful and added more squiggles to the record. "We have multiple names, too, like you do. Here are my other names, Jean and Roy. I used to get teased at school, because Roy is our family name, but it's also used as a name for boys. And on top of that, Jean spelled differently is a boy's name. I guess Tama is kind of odd in itself. Most people would use either Tammy or Tamara."

The reminiscing seemed to calm her, but her shoulders slumped, reminding me of the sadness she'd been showing when we arrived at this abandoned camp.

"I suppose I'd better get to work on the air conditioning around here," I announced gruffly. "Looks like you're about to start leaking. And you haven't finished your story."

"Finished? That's the whole thing. Aren't three names enough?"

"You left out the most important explanation. What's so funny about being Haillyen?"

She did laugh then, a combination of our rumbly belly-bellow and her natural high-pitched trills. "Oh, yes, I can't leave that out, can I? It's just that it sounds like a word in my language, the word that means an utterly bizarre, strange creature. Sometimes it just means a person from another country. But we also use it to mean someone from another planet, an outer-space invader . . . or a creature from another universe." She laughed again, a little more restrainedly, and wiped her eyes on her sleeve. "You see? It's what I am, isn't it? It's what we are to each other. It's just too funny for mere words. I wouldn't change it for the world."

Then she wrapped both arms around me in a fierce hug that threatened to wrench my third dorsal spine. But I responded in kind, my long azure tentacles wrapping around her tightly, so that I could feel her pulse rattling behind those fragile ribs. I'm not sure what finally prompted us to let go. Perhaps the cawing bird had made one of his complaints, because just as I lifted my head, I saw the pest swoop across the clearing and take off into the sky.

"Well," she sniffed. "Good luck with the air-conditioning problem. Make sure you put my name on all those papers."

"I will," I said, struggling with this sense of finality, irritated with the distractions of a chilly breeze rolling across the ridge and the chatter of a dozen bird calls. "Come back."

But she only laughed, very softly and gently. "No, no. What you say, where I come from, is *hyoo awl kum baknaow, yaheer?* And then I say, I say, um, *seeya layder el-legaydr.*" Then she reached out, and formally brushed my chest with her fingertips. "Fare you well, Varayla Ansegwe. Give my love to Kantalare and to silly old Jemenga."

Automatically, I returned the gesture. But all my plans to overcome her objections were crumbling in the face of ritual and reality. She knew. Haillyen had known all along I would try to challenge her at this point. And K'alare *was* waiting for me, back at the little pond, still expecting me to return before nightfall.

Was I really expecting to traipse after Haillyen without her consent, like a stray animal lost in the woods? How would I fare, the lone real person in a universe of squeaky Stick Men? There would be no guarantee of return; indeed, most likely I would never see my beloved again. I stared down at Haillyen, knowing full well that she was reading me like a sentimental video.

She had always seemed so small, so fragile.

And then I suffered one last dizzying perception shift: Haillyen … Tama? … was small, yes, but she was tough. She'd survived contact with a creature that killed my people with a simple hello. She had sought and obtained help from another group of completely alien creatures. At every turn, she learned what she needed to survive. She didn't faint at the sight of strangeness. Most of all, she didn't thrive in the comfort of a tiny country cottage.

I thought ruefully of all the extra gear in the pack I'd swung on so lightly that morning. And I set aside all the lurid arguments I'd worked out in the depths of the long night. I ventured only the quietest heartfelt plea. "I would go with you, if only you'd say yes. We would manage. I could help, you know I could. K'alare would understand."

But she only looked back at me with those shining wet eyes and shook her head firmly in the one gesture I'd learned all too well. It was the last thing she asked of me: to let go of my vain attempt to be her rescuer one more time.

"Then go in light, Varayla Haillyen," I said at last, adding, "Don't forget. The Family remembers."

The tears were coursing down like rain now. She didn't bother to try wiping them away. I knew I was paler than the hazy sky above, but I didn't regret that she saw and understood. She lifted her pack, hopped over the streamlet, and strode up the trail.

I watched her familiar, two-footed progress up the slope. When she was about to step into the shadow of the next patch of trees, I trumpeted my fingers and called out "Hey! *Hyoo awl kum baknaow, yaheer?*"

The distant figure stopped and waved. Perhaps she hollered back, but the wind was against her. She disappeared under the trees.

I worked on the poem all the way back to our little camp. The tone of the piece had changed; it no longer served as a romantic paean to the natural beauty of the wilderness. When I finally came in sight of the pond, I paused for a moment. K'alare was moving silently, intently at the water's edge, her golden arms stretching and weaving over the sunlit pool as she filled her little glass vials with pondwater and microbes. The light flowed over her like cold fire, and my heart stood still.

# ABOUT THE AUTHOR

Vanessa MacLaren-Wray writes science fiction and fantasy exploring the challenges of communication and attachment in a diverse, complex universe. She's the author of the Patchwork Universe series, including *All That Was Asked,* "The True Son," and *Shadows of Insurrection.* She's a member of the Truck Stop at the Center of the Galaxy consortium, with "Coke Machine" and *The Smugglers.* Her short fiction has appeared with Dragon Gems and in the award-winning anthology *Fault Zone: Reverse.* She hosts regular online open mics for the California Writers Club and acts as a guest host for the podcast *Small Publishing in a Big Universe.* She is also an active member of the Science Fiction and Fantasy Writers of America (SFWA).

As an energy systems engineer, she has analyzed electric power systems, studied climate-safe technology, and written extensively on energy issues. The oddball robots she builds out of kids' toys and stray parts do not seek to destroy humans—instead, they brew tea and play music. Vanessa lives in farm country, where fields of strawberries and artichokes hold the developers at bay. When not arguing with her cats, she works on new stories, her email journal *Messages from the Oort Cloud*, and her website, *Cometary Tales (cometarytales.com).* Find all her connections at *linktr.ee/Vanessa_MacLarenWray.*

# ALSO IN THIS SERIES

## THE TRUE SON
A STORY OF THE UNREMEMBERED KING

by Vanessa MacLaren-Wray

*As foster-son to the king, Corren's technically a candidate for the kingship, a position filled only at the discretion of the matriarchs of Jeska. He doesn't want the job.*

## SHADOWS OF INSURRECTION
THE UNREMEMBERED KING: BOOK ONE

by Vanessa MacLaren-Wray

*Once in a generation, the matriarchs of Jeska choose a new king to manage the government and command the Guard — protecting Jeskans from crime, invaders, and insurgency.*

Available from Water Dragon Publishing in
hardcover, trade paperback, and digital editions
*waterdragonpublishing.com*

# ALSO BY THE AUTHOR

## PARRISH BLUE

by Vanessa MacLaren-Wray

*Sallie never expected to discover a world she'd forgotten how to imagine.*

## COKE MACHINE

**FROM THE "TRUCK STOP AT THE CENTER OF THE GALAXY"**

by Vanessa MacLaren-Wray

*Every truck stop needs a coke machine.*

## THE SMUGGLERS

**FROM THE "TRUCK STOP AT THE CENTER OF THE GALAXY"**

by Vanessa MacLaren-Wray

*Attachment is everything.*

Available from Water Dragon Publishing in
hardcover, trade paperback, and digital editions
*waterdragonpublishing.com*

# YOU MIGHT ALSO ENJOY

## MEMORY AND METAPHOR
by Andrea Monticue

*Civilization fell. It rose.*

*At some point, people built starships.*

## SNAIL'S PACE
by Susan McDonough-Wachtman

*Orphaned and penniless in Hong Kong in 1884 —
what's a young gentlewoman to do?*

## THE WORLD'S SHATTERED SHELL
by Laurence Raphael Brothers

*It's the end of the Age of Kali and our world is dying,
its bounds shrunken to encompass a single city.*

Available from Water Dragon Publishing in
hardcover, trade paperback, and digital editions
*waterdragonpublishing.com*